The Hounds
of
Hollenbeck

MAX GRIFFIN

THE HOUNDS OF HOLLENBECK
Copyright © 2015 MAX GRIFFIN
ISBN 978-1-61292-137-2
ISBN 10: 161292137X
Cover Art Designed by Anastasia Rabiyah
Edited by Cassi Reed and Jessica Glanville

Published by Purple Sword Publications, LLC
Tucson, Arizona, USA
www.PurpleSword.com

Dedication:

E. Poe Ferguson

Chapter 1

Saturday, October 6

Sam leaned against the wall of the Tool Box, one of only three gay bars in Hollenbeck, and tried to ignore the rockabilly music that thundered from the speakers hanging over the dance floor. Disco lights whirled across a dozen guys pirouetting with each other, while at least a hundred more jammed every corner of the bar. He longed for the quiet jazz place he'd frequented in Los Angeles and once again questioned the wisdom of moving here. Maybe he'd over-rated the chance to earn his masters in criminology at Browning College.

He sighed and scanned the crowd. It was the same tiresome mix of cowboy queens, muscle boys, and yuppie clones as every other night. That skinny blond huddled in the corner was the only one who appeared remotely interesting. With his spiky hair and serious blue eyes, he looked like he'd be more at home in a library or a science lab. He was cute, sure, but it was that air of intellectual innocence that made Sam want to get into his head.

He pushed away from the wall to make his move, but some Izod-wearing pseudo-preppy chose that instant to latch onto his target. Sam frowned as a tipsy muscle boy with no shirt jostled him, but he kept his gaze on those grave, crystalline eyes that had first caught his attention. A nervous grin flickered on the blond's face as the preppy clone chatted him up. Sam chewed his lower lip. It looked like another lonely Saturday night after all. He returned to his perch against the wall.

When his cell phone buzzed, he was almost glad for the interruption. He recognized the dispatch number for the Hollenbeck Police Department. It wasn't his shift, so why were they calling? He punched answer, held one hand over his right ear and the phone to his left ear. "Sondergard here."

"Sam, that you?" Chief Hartman's voice crackled from the phone.

Of course it's me, you idiot. "Yes, sir. What's up?" He kept his voice respectful.

"What's that racket? Where you at?"

Great. The last thing he needed was to out himself to that homophobe Hartman. They couldn't fire him for being gay, but they could sure make his life miserable. "I'm at a party, sir. Let me step outside." Sam maneuvered through the gyrating male torsos and angled toward the entrance.

"Yeah, whatever. Look, patrol's found a body out by the old lawn mower factory."

"A body, sir?" Sam's skin prickled. The music still thumped from the interior of the bar after the door slammed behind him, but he no longer needed to plug his right ear. He hitched his leather motorcycle jacket tighter against the chilly night air and headed toward his aging Honda.

"Yeah. Looks like it's been there for a while. If you ask me, this is just some homeless faggot who offed himself with drugs. Just the kind of thing you used to work in LA. I want you on the case, Sondergard. The Mayor don't want no bad press."

Sam rolled his eyes. Saying homeless people "offed themselves" blamed them for their situation, as if they chose to be poor. Besides, he could care less what the city's publicity hound of a mayor wanted. Patience. Sam kept his voice steady. "Yes, sir. Where did you say this was, again?" He fished his keys out of his pocket and opened his car trunk.

"I told you, the old lawn mower factory. It's off of Jenkins Avenue, not far from the Eagles Cemetery."

"Sir, I've only been in town six months. Can you give me the address?" Sam pulled his weapon from the kit in the trunk, belted it on and hung his badge and ID on a strap around his neck. His backup pistol was already strapped to his ankle.

The Chief huffed, but then said, "2183 Geary Street. How soon can you be there?"

Sam settled into the driver's seat and punched the address into his GPS. "Sixteen minutes. Who's the officer at the scene?"

"Cliff Murdock. The Medical Examiner's on his way."

Murdock. He was young, but a good cop. Sam started his car. "I'm on my way, sir."

"Good. I'll expect a report first thing in the morning. Say nine AM. Wrap it up nice and clean, you hear me?"

Sam looked at his phone. The jerk had hung up without waiting for an answer. He was better than the mayor, but they were both hacks. Unprofessional. That masters degree had better be worth it. He couldn't get out of small town politics soon enough.

Away from the isolated night spots like the Tool Box, Hollenbeck turned into a ghost town by eleven o'clock most nights, even Saturdays. After Sam crossed the railroad tracks that marked the transition to the old industrial heart of the city, the only vehicle he passed was a rattle-trap of a van that spewed foul exhaust. It disappeared into a side street next to a boarded-up warehouse as Sam sped by. Twelve blocks to go.

A black-and-white police cruiser was parked in an alley at the address, the flash of its lightbar chasing red-hued shadows into the depths of the alley. Sam pulled up behind, blinked his lights and called dispatch. "Sondergard here. Can you tell Murdock I'm at the scene?" Best to check in rather than surprise him.

"Will do, Sam."

From the sound of her voice, it must be Karen running dispatch tonight. "Thanks. Anything else for me?"

"I've called for a wagon, but they were out for a fender bender. It'll be about thirty minutes before they get there. That okay?"

"Yeah. The ME's not here yet, either. That it?"

"Yeah. The asshole said he had to finish his hand at the club. It's poker night, you know."

"Just so he keeps his priorities straight. Thanks, Karen. I know you do what you can. Sondergard out."

He stepped out of his car as Murdock approached, carrying a clipboard. Sam spoke first. "Hey, Cliff. What do you have?"

Cliff's eyes locked onto Sam, and his fingers twitched although his voice was rock solid. "It's some kid, Sam. A boy, from the clothes, but it's hard to tell. The decomp is pretty advanced."

Sam frowned. Cliff wasn't a rookie, but DBs weren't exactly routine in Hollenbeck. He sounded steady enough, though. "It's been here long enough to decompose? In the middle of town? And no one reported it?"

Cliff shrugged. "Ain't like anybody comes here to work no more. This part of town's been pretty much abandoned since the Crash. I stopped because I thought I saw a light inside the building. Weren't nothing, but when I got out, I caught a whiff. Decomp's hard to miss, once you've smelled it."

"So, can you show me the scene?"

"Sure. Ain't much to see." Cliff led Sam deeper into the alley. "It smells pretty bad."

"Be patient and try to breathe normal, through your nose. It'll numb your olfactory glands in a few minutes, and then it won't be near so bad." Sam braced himself. Advanced decomp was always bad.

Uncollected trash piled high against the brick walls on each side of them, and the stench was unmistakable. A pathetic heap of bloated, decaying flesh and tattered clothing lay under the loading dock at the end of the alley. Cliff illuminated the scene with his flashlight, while Sam circled the body snapping pictures with his cell phone. Flies buzzed around the corpse, and beetles scuttled away from the light.

"You move anything?" Sam asked.

Cliff shook his head. "No, sir. I know better."

"Good man." He knelt next to the body and examined his jacket. "This looks like a letter jacket. Orange and black. That tell you anything?"

"Them's the colors of OSU, over in Corvalis."

"I was thinking more of a local school." He turned his attention to the victim's legs. The blue jeans were torn and something had ripped them open at mid-thigh. He peered closer. It looked like there was a *bite* missing out of the kid's leg muscle. What would do that?

Cliff shuffled his feet. "Halsted uses those colors, too." He named a small town about twenty miles away.

"Well then, if he doesn't have an ID, that might help identify him." Footfalls sounded from the street, and both men whirled to face the sound.

A heavy baritone called out. "Anybody there?"

"Detective Sergeant Sam Sondergard. Who are you?"

"Doctor Forrest Twilling. The ME." A tall, spare man with a halo of thinning white hair coalesced from the shadows, backlit by the strobe of the red lights on the cruiser.

5

He clutched at his sport coat and pinched his features into a greeting. "Damned cold out here. Stinks to high heaven, too. The Chief seemed to think this wash...was...important enough to call me away from my poker game at the club."

Sam let him approach. Sure enough, he reeked of alcohol. This just kept getting better and better. "We've got a dead body, male, late teens or early twenties. From the state of decomp, it looks like he's been here a few weeks."

Twilling waved a hand under his nose. "Phew. They could have warned me about the stench." He held a handkerchief over his face. "Can't tell much. Probably some homeless kid who ODed on drugs."

Sam controlled his annoyance. "Maybe. Maybe not." He pointed to the leg injury. "What's that?"

Twilling scowled at him, but then peered at the body. "I'm not sure." He knelt, pulled out a ball-point pen from his jacket pocket, and probed. "It looks like an animal got to the body. Those are bite marks on the bone." He stood. "There are lots of stray dogs around here. The city really needs to do a better job with animal control."

Drunk or not, at least he looked at the body. The LAPD would have had a full CID team here, but Hollenbeck was too small and too broke for that. Sam really should call in the state police. He quirked his lips. Like *that* was going to happen. The chief would go ballistic over the bad publicity. He turned back to Twilling. "I thought it might be an animal bite, too. Postmortem or perimortem?"

The physician shrugged. "Really, who knows with the shape the body's in? Microscopy might tell us something, but why bother?"

Sam snapped, "Because he's dead, and he deserves answers. Like any human being."

Twilling stood and glared at Sam, but the ambulance crew chose that moment to enter the alley. He scowled at Sam

6

while the EMTs wheeled a stretcher toward the body. "If you need a release, Detective...*Sondergard*, is it?"

"Yes, sir." Yelling at the ME wasn't smart, not if he wanted to solve this case. "I'm sorry sir. I know your job is difficult, and you want to solve this as much as I do. I shouldn't have snapped at you."

Twilling waved a casual hand at him. "Forgiven. Forgotten. It'sh...it's late, and I'm sure you don't want to be here either. In any case, you have my official release of the body. Is there something I need to sign?"

Murdock flipped to a form on his clipboard and held it out for Twilling to sign.

"There you go. I can't tell anything more here. I'm returning to the club. You'll have your autopshy...autopsy...in due course." He stalked away.

Sam watched him until he vanished around the corner, and then turned to Cliff. "Good work to have the forms ready. Thank you."

The officer grinned like a puppy getting a treat. "Thanks, Sam. I try to be prepared."

"Well, you handled it better than I did. Thank you." He turned to the EMTs. "Can you folks wait a minute? I want to examine the body and check for ID."

The lead tech shrugged. "Sure, officer." She tipped her head at the body. "We'll need a shovel to get this one in a body bag. It's bound to come apart."

Sam knelt next to the body and waved flies away from his face. The stink didn't seem as bad. The trick he'd learn from the assistant ME in LA was working: his olfactory glands were numb.

The Chief might be an idiot, but he had been right about one thing. Sam had seen far too many scenes this bad or worse when he was with the LAPD. They still got to him. His nose could turn numb, but never his heart. He turned to the medics. "You got some latex gloves you can spare?" He had them in his kit, but didn't feel like walking back to his car.

"Sure." She opened a pouch on the stretcher and handed Sam a packet.

He snapped them on and gently tilted the body to one side, trying to ignore the squishy sounds the remains made as they oozed to a new position. No ID in the jeans' pockets. Nothing in the letter jacket, either, but it did say Halsted Beavers on the back. That was something, at least. He looked again at the kid's head. "Hey." He paused to read the medic's name tag. "Susan, take a look at this, will you?" He point to a wound in the body's head. "What's that look like to you?"

She squatted next to him and extended her hand to Cliff. "Can I borrow your light?" She shined it onto the wound in the skull and poked a latex-clad finger two knuckles deep into the head. "Something or someone hit him pretty hard, Detective. Hard enough to crack his skull and kill him, if that was antemortem."

"Yeah, that's what I thought, too." The ME would probably be able to tell more on autopsy. "Okay, I'm finished. Go ahead and transport him."

He stood next to Cliff and peeled off the gloves. "We should work the scene, even though I doubt we find anything. He's been lying here for weeks. Still, maybe we'll turn something up, some clue as to what happened."

"Whatever you say, Detective." Cliff's voice trembled. His eyes bulged as the EMTs began to scoop the remains into a body bag. "Uh, I think I'm going — " He bolted to the front of the alley and the sounds of vomiting filled the air.

Sue glanced up and chuckled. "Get's 'em every time."

Sam waited a moment before approaching Cliff. "Don't worry, man. It happens to everyone. You did good work tonight."

Cliff stood and wiped his mouth. "God. He was just a kid. And now — " He stopped for a round of dry heaves. When he was done, he turned stricken features toward Sam. "Detective, I'm sorry. That was unprofessional. How do you get *used* to things like that?"

"Cliff, if you got used to it, I wouldn't want you as a fellow police officer. You never get used to it. You learn to control your reactions some, but you never get used to it."

"What you think happened to him, Sam?"

"Hard to say. But I don't think he ODed. There's no works here--no needles, no syringes, no baggies. No evidence at all of drugs. And there's that hole in his skull. I think we've got ourselves a homicide."

"But he was just a kid. Who would kill a kid?"

"I don't know, but I'm going to find out." Sam wanted a cigarette, despite having quit over a year ago. "I'll tell you this, though. I'm afraid this might not be an isolated case."

Cliff's eyes widened. "What you mean? We haven't had anything like this in Hollenbeck ever, as far as I know."

"Right. But I've been reviewing open cases since I got here. Missing person's cases in particular. There's over a dozen of them in the last thirty-six months, including surrounding communities. They all involve young men in their late teens and early twenties."

"Runaways." Cliff's tone was dismissive.

"Some of them, maybe. That's what the case files say. But that's a lot of missing kids, and all with the same basic profile. They even look kind of alike. Thin, blond hair, same approximate age. At least five or six had been kicked out of their homes for being gay. It wouldn't be the first time a predator targeted vulnerable gay kids."

"Jeeze, you mean like that Dahmer guy? Right here in Hollenbeck? I can't believe it."

Sam chewed the side of his cheek and thought about the hole in the victim's thigh. Like the ME, he'd thought it was an animal bite, but maybe it was something else. Still, no reason to be an alarmist. "Probably not. Serial killers are pretty rare." Even so, they could be anywhere, including here. After all, he'd learned in class that the FBI estimated there were between twenty and fifty serial killers active in the US at any given time.

Sam slapped Cliff on the back. "Whatever happened, this kid deserves our best, right? The EMTs are done, so let's take this place apart. Maybe we'll find a clue." Serial killer or not, something wasn't right here. There were too many missing person's cases and they were too similar for pure coincidence.

Sam thought of the guys at the Tool Box earlier tonight. His victim could have been dancing and having fun at the bar a few short weeks ago. Shit, the next victim could be *Sam*, or that cute spiky-haired guy he'd watched from afar. He was the right type that was for sure. The homophobic city administration, from the mayor to the chief, would hate it, but he wasn't going to let this drop. He couldn't.

Chapter 2

Monday, October 8

Allen's sneakers squeaked against the polished terrazzo flooring of the post-modern lab that housed Browning College's Army CHIP contract. He stopped at the stainless steel door to the kennel that was the heart of the project and punched in his security code. His heart lifted at the cacophony of cheery doggy banter that greeted him on the other side.

Allen didn't care how valuable or dangerous these animals were, dogs should be kept outside, not in a sterile lab. Half a dozen cages lined each side of the kennel like jail cells. The dogs yipped in their joy at seeing him, standing with their forepaws on the stainless steel bars of their enclosures. Allen grinned back and wished he could free them all.

Allen walked through the kennel, stopping at each cage and greeting each animal. Officially, they only had numbers, but he'd named every one of them. They all looked pretty much alike, but not to Allen. Sure, they were almost-but-not quite golden retrievers. Silver flecks marred their yellow fur, and their heads were outsize for breed standard. Not surprising, since they were a new breed altogether, genetically engineered for the Army. They weren't even dogs, at least not entirely. They were super-dogs, canine Einsteins.

The smartest, subject CHIP.13.5, could understand over three thousand words. When he finally arrived at her cage, she gave him a woebegone look. *Arf?*

Allen was sure her bark was a question, probably asking where he'd been. "Teena! How's my best girl?" He knelt next to her and let her sniff at his outstretched hand. "I bet you'd like a treat, wouldn't you, Teena?" He'd named her after her generation number, thirteen.

She wagged her tail and nodded her head up and down, her eyes riveted on her best friend. *Woof!*

He pulled a doggie snack from the stash in his pocket and held it through bars. Her tongue slipped the morsel from his palm, and she hunkered down to crunch on it. He waited for her to finish and then let her sniff his fingers again. Finished with her greeting, she sat on her haunches, her tail thumping in glee. Her brown eyes never left him, as if waiting to find what her pal wanted to do today. She pressed her nose through the bars and nuzzled at the pants pocket where Allen stashed her treats.

He tousled her ears through the cage. "No more treats for now, girl." She might never win a dog show, but that didn't matter to Allen. To him, she was beautiful and smarter than any dog who had ever lived. Best of all, she loved him for what he was. Skinny, geeky, spiky hair all a-tangle--none of that mattered to her.

Memories of being dumped last Saturday night at the Tool Box made his mouth turn down. Why had that guy hit on him if he was just going to walk away without explanation? Was he that unattractive?

The lab door opened, breaking his reverie. Good thing. Self-pity never got anyone anything.

"Allen, honey, what you doing here so early?" Trish Samson, a sturdy, middle-aged African-American woman, stood in the doorway in her pink lab scrubs. "Tell me you had a date this weekend."

His face heated. He stood and averted his eyes. "No date. I'm a perpetual lonely heart."

"Sweetie, you ain't never going to get a boyfriend with that attitude." She scowled at him. "You got to try, you hear me?"

"I do." He hated the whiny tone of his voice. Why couldn't he be more confident and masculine, like those guys at the bar?

"I suppose you went cruising again. Did you go to that *bar*? Child, that's not safe. Edna Willoughby told me at church that her cousin went to that den of sin, and now he's done disappeared. No one knows where he's at." She put her hands on her hips. "And he's not the only one I've heard about. There was this nice boy from over in Halsted who was in our Bible study — "

Allen held up his hands, palm forward. "Okay, okay already. I'm safe, believe me. No one even looks at me. Besides, I'm busy with classes and our work here. I don't need a boyfriend."

Her eyes softened. "Everyone needs someone to care for them, hon. You should come to my church. We're open and affirming, and there's some *nice* boys there."

A Baptist revival was the last thing Allen wanted. "I'll think about it, I promise." He also didn't want to hurt Trish's feelings. Time to change the subject. "What brings you in so early on a Monday morning? I've got some protocols to run before class this afternoon." Hey tilted an eyebrow at her. "I thought lab techs kept regular hours, not like us lowly graduate students."

She snapped her gloves in place and opened a supply cabinet next to the door. "I've got some bloodwork for the good Dr. Sarnok: a CBC on specimen 12.6 by 9 AM sharp, or he'll have my be-hind."

Allen cast a wary glance at the door. "Dr. Sarnok's here this morning?" Allen had hoped to evade the man's poison tongue for at least one day at the lab.

"He's prowling around. You watch yourself, you hear? You know he eats doctoral students for breakfast."

"I guess I better get busy then." He reached for the latch on the cage. Maybe he could escape with Teena to the test range before Sarnok had a chance to slam him over some imagined failing.

"Hey! What you doing?" Trish pointed to a sign on the wall. Notices about animal safety plastered the walls of the lab: precautions about leashes and warnings to be alert for violent behaviors. "Put the leash on her first, okay?"

"Teena would never hurt anyone."

Her face softened. "I know that, child. But after that incident three years ago, Dr. Harzig's been nervous as cat in room full of rocking chairs." She pointed to the surveillance camera hanging near the ceiling in one corner. "He'll fire your ass if he catches you breaking protocol, don't matter how cute it is."

Harzig was the staff veterinarian. Allen snorted. "He's no threat. I'm more worried about him *grabbing* my ass than firing it."

"True that. He's kind of creepy, that one."

"Besides, there's not been an incident in three years, not since Dr. Sarnok reduced the non-canine genetic material in the dogs."

"You just follow the rules, y'hear?" She turned her back and pulled supplies from the cabinets.

He grinned and winked at Teena. "Shall we get some work done, girl?"

Her tail stopped thumping, and her head shook the other way, an emphatic no. She licked at his hand again and nuzzled through the cage at the pocket with the treats.

"Not now, Teena. After we finish our tests, then you can have another treat."

She looked at him, her head tipped to one side. Then she woofed, nodded her head, and signaled readiness for the task ahead.

"That's a good dog." He hooked the leash through her collar and then opened the cage. "Okay, girl, we'll go outside, and you can play for a bit before we get to work."

Her ears perked up, and she padded to the door to the lab, Allen following. She led Allen down the hallway toward the experimental test range. She cast from one side of the hall to the other, nose to the floor, stopping now and then to sniff out some interesting new odor. Allen waited for his friend to satisfy her curiosity. "Don't take too long, Teena. We've got lots of work to do today."

An older man dressed in a prim, creased white lab coat entered from a side corridor and blocked their way. "Hello Mr. LeClerc." He peered into his phone without look up. He was handsome enough to be an aging movie star, with the precise diction of a Shakespearean actor. Gray flecked the temples of his flaxen hair, and his shoes probably cost more than Allen made in a month. A delicate scent of cologne hovered about him.

Allen's heart sank, and he mumbled, "Hello, Dr. Sarnok." His short, skinny build, worn blue jeans, T-shirts, and spiky hair always made him feel like a stick figure around his glamorous adviser. He braced himself for the inevitable scolding. Everything he did was always wrong. Except breathing. His advisor had never complained about how Allen breathed. Yet.

Allen jerked at Teena's leash, and edged down the hallway toward the door to the test range. Maybe he could still escape.

"What tests are you running today, Allen?" Sarnok continued to flip through screens.

Too late. "We're going to do a couple of the new search protocols today, sir. Eighteen Bee and Cee if we have time." Teena sniffed at Sarnok's shoes, her tail wagging. "Teena! Stop that!"

Sarnok finally looked up. "Mr. LeClerc. That is an experimental animal." He stooped and tugged at the red tag clipped to her ear. "CHIP.13.5." Sarnok pronounced it "chip dot thirteen dot five." The same code was tattooed to her other ear.

"I know. I'm sorry, Dr. Sarnok." Shit. He didn't even know what he'd done wrong and already he was apologizing.

"You know it is not good to anthropomorphize these specimens. They are neither our pets nor our friends. They are CHIPs, Canine-Human Inter-genetic Prototypes."

That again. God, could he be more of an asshole? Be careful, though. He can screw you. "I know that, sir. I'll try to do better." Teena tugged at her leash, tracking some new scent down the hall, jerking Allen's arm about. He snapped on the leash, wishing for the power to make Sarnok go away, like the little boy in *The Twilight Zone* episode. Then it really would be a good life, or at least a better one.

Sarnok sneered at him. "See that you do." His grim gaze glowered over his glasses. "If you don't have proper scientific detachment, your results won't be valid."

"I understand, Dr. Sarnok."

"If your results are not valid, then your dissertation won't be valid." He licked his lips with a thin smile. "We wouldn't want that to happen, now would we, Mr. LeClerc?"

Allen flushed. "No sir, not at all, sir." What an eff-ing bully. It was too late to choose a new advisor. Allen was screwed no matter what.

"Just so we understand each other." Without another word, Sarnok pivoted and walked away.

Teena stood still, her head tipped to one side, looking back and forth between Allen and the departing Sarnok. She whimpered and planted a doggie kiss on Allen's hand.

He chewed his lip and forced a grin. "Don't worry, girl. He can't really do anything to us."

She considered that for a moment, nodded her head, sniffed, and put her nose to the floor. She was off again, on an endless doggie quest for new smells. Allen let her lead him the rest of the way down the hall and out the door to the test range.

Once in the fenced area outside, he released her, sat on the grass, and watched while she romped, scouting out new smells. He knew Sarnok would disapprove, but Teena hated being in the cage and so loved being outdoors. It wouldn't hurt to let her have some fun before running the protocols. She was a good dog and was always diligent with the tests. She liked puzzling out the scents and clues and finding the right trail. Allen knew this was due to a combination of instinct and engineering, but he was sure at least some of her joy in the running tests derived from pleasing her friend Allen.

****

At noon Allen walked from the lab to the main campus, the morning's test results stuffed into his battered briefcase. He didn't rate an office at the gleaming CHIP facility and instead had a cubbyhole in the attic of the old Zoology Building. As he passed by the Union, he decided to have lunch in the cafeteria.

He wove his way through the crowds of jabbering undergraduates, juggling his tray and his briefcase. At the front of dining area, some Navy ROTC cadets sat in their crisp white uniforms at three tables they had pushed together. Allen's eyes locked with one good looking cadet who had a dark tan and piercing blue eyes. He was familiar, somehow. Then Allen had it: the cadet was the guy who had bought him a beer at the Tool Box last Saturday night before dumping him. Pete, that was his name. Pete caught Allen's gaze, his face flushed, and he lowered his eyes to his half-eaten burger.

Allen looked away. Fantastic. Now I've been rejected in the Union, too.

Three coeds vacated a table in a far corner, and he dashed to it. He swept aside the newspapers and plates they had left behind and wedged the contents from his tray onto the table. He loaded his now empty tray with the mess the coeds left behind and snaked his way back through jammed tables to the waste bin on the far side of the room.

Just as he dumped the tray, someone else put their tray on his table. His heart sank as he fought his way back through the crowd to confront the table thief. "Excuse me." He stood over the usurper and cleared his throat.

The young man looked up at him, and an impossible, infectious grin burst across his face. "I'm sorry, I saw you come in and it looked like you were alone, too. It's so friggin' crowded in here. Do you mind if we share?" He wiped his hands on his napkin and stood. "I'm Sam, by the way." He stuck out his hand.

Allen accepted it out of reflex. "I'm Allen." His gaze roamed around the room and then returned to the other's handsome face. He had a neat goatee, and from the stubble on his cheeks it looked like he hadn't shaved today. His dark, almond-shaped eyes loomed over with his sunny smile. Something mysterious lurked there. Something deep and alluring. Allen repressed a tingle in his loins. "It is crowded. Glad to share. Nice to meet you." Another good looking guy, another chance to be rejected. The story of Allen's life.

Sam stripped off his black leather jacket and plopped back down in his chair, muscles flexing on his arms. "That's great. I really appreciate it." He took an immense bite out of his hamburger. "These frigging freshmen really get on my nerves, y'know?"

Allen slipped into his seat. Sam wore a tight-fitting black t-shirt that exposed his lithe form to perfection. No one had a right to be this sexy. Allen was glad that the table hid his physical reaction. This guy had ebony hair, buzzed short to his scalp, and muscles on his muscles. Allen was sure he'd seen him someplace before, but he couldn't quite place where. Careful, boy. He's probably straight and would beat you up if he knew how turned on you are.

Allen lowered his gaze. "I know exactly what you mean, about the freshman I mean. Entitled. Always babbling and pushing. Superficial and self-centered." He stirred his soup.

Sam used a French fry as a ketchup shovel. "You must be a graduate student too? I'm a first year criminology student."

So they hadn't met in class. "I'm a doctoral student in Zoology." Allen's heart quickened. The discomfort that always plagued him while talking to a good looking guy washed over him.

"Wow, a doctoral student. I'm impressed." Sam chewed on a wad of fries. "I'm just working on a lowly masters. I think I'd like to work for VICAP, with the FBI. You know, profile serial killers and the like. How about you?"

"I'm working with the CHIP project. It's a big Army contract that Dr. Sarnok has."

Sam nodded. "Oh yeah, I think I heard of it. Seems to me I know someone who works in the zoo department. Lizzie Bateman. Maybe you know her?"

Allen's heart sank. So, he's straight after all. "Sorry, no. Is she your girlfriend?"

That got him a strange look. "Not hardly." Sam took another hefty chunk out of his hamburger. "Say, haven't I seen you around? Maybe at the Tool Box?"

Allen's face flushed, and he averted his eyes. "Maybe."

"Yeah, yeah. I'm sure I saw you there last Saturday night. I was going to ask you to dance, but I got called away." More hamburger disappeared into his mouth.

No one ever asked Allen to dance. Ever. "Really? I wish you had hung around. One guy bought me a beer, but I guess I wasn't his type. I wasn't with anyone." *Shit! What am I doing? He's way out of my league.* He remembered now. He had seen Sam staring at him from across the bar when Pete had been not-hitting on him.

"Well, I wish I could have hung around. Now that we've met, I bet we'd have fun together." He drained half his soda. "Look, I'm late for class, but I'd really like to get to know you better." He pulled a card from his jacket and scrawled on the back. "Give me a call, okay? I'm not working this weekend, so maybe we can we can go out for a show or dinner or something."

Allen gave him stunned stare. With trembling fingers he slipped the card into his shirt pocket. "I'd like that." He opened his briefcase, tore out a sheet of notepaper, and scrawled his name and cell phone number on it. "Here's my number. You can call me anytime, okay?"

Sam swiped at his mouth with his napkin, having made his meal vanish. He creased the paper and stuffed it into his jacket. "You can count on it, Allen." He flashed another of those dazzling grins while he slipped into his jacket. He bussed his dishes and strode away.

Allen pulled Sam's card from his pocked and scanned it. Adrenalin tingled through the fingertips that clutched at the card. In neat letters it announced, "Sam Sondergard, Detective Sergeant First Class, Hollenbeck Police Department."

He's just made a date with a cop. How hot was that?

Chapter 3

One AM Tuesday, October 9

Bobby slouched over the steering wheel and peered out the grime-smeared windshield of his van. Puddles of yellow light from the streetlamps alternated with shadows and stretched to infinity before and after him. He reached out to stroke the scarred head of the mongrel that rested in the passenger seat next to him. "It looks like it's too late to find something to have fun with tonight. What do you think, Spot?"

The dog tipped his too-large head and seemed to consider the question. He put his forepaws on the dashboard and scanned the boarded-up warehouses lining the empty street. Finished with his inspection, he looked back at Bobby and shook his head no. His tongue flopped out of his mouth over enormous, yellow teeth. Drool leaked onto the van's ragged upholstery.

"Yeah, I guess you're right." Disappointment dragged at Bobby. "We don't have anything better to do, though. May as well keep cruising."

Spot responded with a happy *woof,* and stuck his head out the passenger window.

Bobby ran his palm over the stubble that bristled on his sunken cheeks. He pushed greasy ropes of dark hair back onto his balding head and reached out to pet his dog. His hands were filthy, and grime fouled his untrimmed fingernails, but Spot didn't care. He would do anything Bobby asked.

Under the mud matting the animal's shanks, his fur was mostly yellow, but flecked with traces of gray. One ear flopped in two pieces from an old injury. A faded tattoo reading 2.1 marred the other ear. The dog was a misshapen, scarred mess, but Bobby loved Spot for what he was, just like Spot loved him. That was what made their relationship successful.

He sighed and wished someone, anyone, would appear on the street. Well, anyone but a cop. He could do without a repeat of the excitement Saturday night, when the cops had found the broken toy he'd dumped at the lawn mower factory. He'd have to go back to using his other location, even if teenagers sometimes showed up for their revolting sexual encounters.

Enough of that. He scanned the street, hoping. Disintegrating warehouses crowded on his left. Brambles and weeds entwined a chain link fence on the right. An old cemetery, dark and silent, lay beyond the fence.

Sometimes he found playthings deep inside the cemetery, near a statue of a grieving monk that stood on a small hillock. It was a pretty good place, one where no one who mattered would see the pickup. Even the statue couldn't see: a shroud of stone cloaked the monk's features, his face forever hidden from view. Crumpled cigarette butts, IV needles and used condoms usually littered the base of the monument, marking it as a meeting place for drug deals and male prostitutes. He grinned. They made good toys, when he could get them.

The blue van wheezed along near the boundary of the cemetery. Now and again the dog's nose twitched as new scents wafted through the night. Eventually, he dropped back inside and woofed at Bobby.

"You found someone for us, Spot?" Bobby practiced his sickly voice, the one that seemed to bubble past a phlegm-congealed throat.

The dog barked, gazing up at his master. His head nodded up and down. Yes. Spot's tail wagged like a crazy metronome. He pawed at the steering wheel. Bobby pulled to the curb and doused the lights. Spot whimpered. The engine stumbled and coughed to a stop.

"Where is he at, Spot?" Anticipation made the hair on his neck prickle. His craving gnawed at him. Insistent, relentless. Lust flamed in his veins.

The dog stood on the seat and pointed his nose toward the cemetery. He tossed his head and woofed again. His eyes reflected the street lamps with a verdant internal gleam.

"There in the cemetery, Spot? He's out there?"

The dog *chuffed* and jerked his head.

Bobby smiled. He reached into the back seat and pulled out a filthy fake cast. He twisted it onto his arm and flexed his hand to make sure it was secure. With a shuddering breath, he opened his door. "Anyone else out there, Spot?"

The dog bounded over him to the street, twitching his nose as he tipped his head this way and that. He peered back at Bobby. This time he shook his head back and forth. No.

Things were looking good. His throat tightened, and visions danced in his head. Intimate visions tinged with blood and sealed with pain. Bobby licked his lips, his tongue passing over a missing eyetooth. Soon. He adjusted his jeans to cloak his desire. Spot ran ahead, leading the way in the murky night.

"Spot! Come back here, dog!" His call wafted through the night, trailing after his mutt. Spot was well trained. Bobby knew he wouldn't answer until they'd completed their mission.

When the statue of the monk loomed out of the darkness, Bobby hid in the shadows. He could just make out a figure huddling there, under the statue, a young man. He was hunkered down, resting with his back against a tombstone. He shivered and clutched at his bright yellow and green letter jacket.

The dog sped forward. He paused at the base of the statue to relieve himself.

"Spot. Where are you, Spot?" Bobby called out, using his feeble old man voice.

The dog scratched at the dirt and sniffed around the base of the statue. He looked directly at the young man and trotted over to him. His tail wagged in frantic swirls.

The young fellow ruffled his ears. "Are you Spot, fella? How ya doin'? Yeah, you're a *good* dog."

Woof! Spot licked at the target's hands and face, accompanied by frenzied tail-wagging. *Woof, woof!*

Time to move in. "Spot! Is that you, dog? Come here, boy. Come to Pappa!" Bobby panted, and clouds of breath puffed from his mouth while he wiped a sheen of cold sweat from his brow.

Spot turned toward his voice and barked.

Bobby wove his way through the shadowy tombstones. As he approached, the scene coalesced out of the darkness and took clearer form. Someone had embroidered the young guy's letter jacket with his name, "Walt Sedgwick." Walt was young and slim, with shaggy hair and a discouraged beard. Dirt smeared his face. As Bobby approached, Walt's stomach rumbled.

Bobby grinned. Good. He's probably desperate, maybe even looking to trick. Well, he's gonna get what he's asking for, and more! A dry chuckle rasped in his throat.

"Hey, mister, didja lose your dog?" Walt's clear tenor rang through the darkness. His voice quivered in the cold.

He'll be fun to play with, all right. Bobby's loins surged, and he fought back against his urgent desire. He stopped short, feigning surprise.

Woof! Spot slobbered ever more frenzied licks onto Walt's hand before stopping and looking at Bobby. The mutt's head bobbed up and down. This was their target, all right.

Bobby plastered his most woebegone look across his face. "Yeah, he's my dog. Spot, come here boy." He dangled the leash. Spot didn't move. He was a smart dog.

Bobby sighed and edged closer. "I was gonna take him for a walk, y'know? To do his business. But he ran off afore I could get his leash on him." He rubbed his cast. "It's hard, what with my arm the way it is."

He'd had to practice to act like a bum, with bad fumbled speech. It was worth it, though. It helped if the target thought Bobby was an ignorant dumbass. He let a smile bend his lips. He'd show them. He *knew* things, intimate things. Soon, Walt would know, too. Bobby couldn't wait see it in his eyes. His eyes would become a window to the divine. Bobby would open the doorway to eternity, but only Walt would pass through.

Walt smiled and tousled the dog's ears again. "I think he already did his business, over there by the statue."

"Okay, that's good." Bobby struggled with the dog's collar. "Could you maybe help me, young fellow? My arm hurts so bad, and I can't get the leash on him. He don't like it much."

"Sure." He took the leash from Bobby and clipped it to the collar. Spot sat on his haunches and looked first at Walt, then the Bobby.

Tension gripped Bobby's gut. Almost there. "I wonder could you please help me get him back into my van? My arm hurts when he tugs at it. It takes two good arms to get him back inside the van."

Walt narrowed his eyes and peered at the older man. He wrinkled his nose. "What's in it for me?"

Bobby suppressed a sneer. *You stink, too, kid.* He calmed himself. *Stay pathetic. Don't spoil it now that you're so close.* "I ain't got no money nor nuthin' to give you, but I'd sure be grateful if you'd help." He paused. *Time for the hook.* "I've got some chips in my van what you could have. Is you cold? I got myself a warm place to sleep, too. Big enough for you to have your own bed." He clutched himself and shuddered.

Walt's stomach growled again, but he still hesitated. The trees rustled in a gust of frigid wind, and his features firmed. With a shrug, he said, "Sure, why not?" He wrapped the leash around his hand. "C'mon, Spot, let's go."

"Oh, thank you so much, young man. It is so good of you to help an old man like me." Bobby rubbed the cast and beamed. Even he could smell the stink of his rotting teeth. It was okay. It would just make him more pitiful and help reel in his latest playmate.

All the way to the van, Bobby babbled about how badly his arm hurt, about how Spot was so hard to handle, about how good it was for Walt to help him.

"Here, let's put him in the back." Bobby rushed ahead and opened the rear door of the van. "If you'll climb inside, then maybe he'll go in after you."

Trash and an overpowering stench clogged the rear of the van. Walt seemed to balk for a moment, but then a frigid gust of wind must have changed his mind. He bit his lip, climbed in, and pulled at the leash. "C'mon Spot, let's go!" The dog resisted a moment and then leaped into the van. His forepaws thrust against Walt's shoulders and delirious licks cascaded across the boy's mouth and cheeks. *Woof!* The two tumbled to the floor, Walt giggling and the dog barking, wagging and licking.

Bobby climbed into the van with them. "I'm so sorry. Spot, what are you doing? Get away from there!" His voice was sharp and biting. Keeping a wary eye on Walt to be sure he wasn't looking, he picked up a crowbar from the clutter on the floor and hid it behind his back.

The dog whimpered and withdrew.

Still laughing, Walt sat up and wiped at his face.

In the streetlight, his cheeks glowed with a perfect, peaches-and-cream complexion. So lovely. So sublime. His flesh cried out for the caress of razor-sharp blades.

Bobby's yearning flared white hot and steel hard. His breath caught in his throat, imagining the first incision. *That* was when those crystalline eyes would speak to him. That moment of epiphany, *that* was what he lived for.

Walt stroked Spot's back. "It's all right. He's just happy to be here I guess."

Bobby edged closer, gazing down at Walt's innocent features. So trusting. Spot crouched and panted, watching, his tongue lolling out of his mouth and slobber pooling in the trash. The dog tipped his head as though to get a better view.

Walt's expression turned cunning, and he touched his crotch. A sly smile bent his lips, and he waggled his hips. Disgusting. What he offered wasn't what Bobby craved. He was just a tramp after all, not the innocent he pretended to be.

He deserved what was going to happen. He was asking for it.

Bobby smiled back, and then, with no warning, swung the crowbar. Walt flopped to the floor of van, blood spouting from a wound in his scalp. The van shook as Bobby swung the crowbar four more times in rapid succession, careful to not to strike the head again. Dropping his weapon, panting, he bound his victim's wrists and ankles with duct tape. One long piece went all the way around Walt's head, muffling his mouth.

Bobby rumpled Spot's ears. "Good dog. We'll have lots of fun with this one. Lots."

Spot nodded in fervid agreement. *Woof!* His tail convulsed with hysterical wags.

Bobby slammed the rear door of the van closed and crawled to the driver's seat, while Spot leaped into the passenger seat. The engine coughed and smoked before it started. Together they drove away, a man, his dog, and their newest playmate.

Chapter 4

Wednesday, October 10

Sam stepped off the elevator into a dingy basement corridor of Hollenbeck Memorial Hospital. Empty beds with rolled-up mattresses lined the scuffed, linoleum floors, and fluorescent lamps hung between exposed ductwork and pipes that cluttered the ceiling. A sign pointed to the way to the morgue.

He traipsed down the hall to a dented stainless steel door marked, "Morgue. Authorized Personnel Only." When he tried the latch, it was locked. Now what? First, Twilling had taken his own sweet time setting up this meeting. Now it was Wednesday, and Sam still didn't have a positive ID on his victim. It wasn't like the ME had any other DBs to handle.

Sam twisted his mouth in disgust, pulled out his phone and sent a text: *It's 7AM. I'm at the Morgue. It's locked.*

A few moments later the door popped open, and the faint scent of formaldehyde and dead body puffed into the hallway. Twilling stood in the entrance, wearing surgical scrubs, gloves, and plastic face guard. "Good morning, Detective."

No apology. Nice. Sam nodded. "Doctor." He followed the ME into the anteroom.

Twilling pointed to lockers and scrubs hanging on one wall. "It's pretty nasty in there, and you won't want the formaldehyde getting in your clothes. It's toxic, you know. I suggest you change before joining me inside."

Sam frowned. "Is that really necessary? I'm used to just wearing a gown."

29

"Up to you, detective. If you were one of my residents, you wouldn't have a choice. I run a tight ship here." His eyes sparked. "Whatever you decide, come inside when you're ready. I've got some interesting findings for you." He opened the heavy freezer-like door that led to the autopsy room and left.

Sam eyed the lockers. The sober Twilling was every bit as much an asshole as the drunk one had been, except that now he at least seemed competent. It couldn't hurt to humor him. Sam stripped off his outer clothes, stashed them in a locker, and pulled on green scrubs, slippers, and a plastic face guard. Feeling silly, he joined the ME.

The morgue itself was kept at reduced pressure, so the smells stayed contained. Sam wrinkled his nose against the mixture of formaldehyde and the stench of a dead body in the putrescent stage. The remains lay under a sheet, exposed from the chest up. The skin was marbled, purplish and black, and the Y-shaped autopsy incision was neatly stitched closed.

Twilling glanced at Sam and nodded. "You're not going to vomit, are you?"

"I've seen worse than this. You said you had findings?"

"Yes. I wish it could have been sooner, but I had an emergency surgery Monday. Living patients have to come first."

Of course, Hollenbeck was too small for a full-time ME. Sam had forgotten that Twilling probably had a private practice with patients to care for. "I understand, Doctor. Show me what you've got." He should be grateful that Twilling seemed to take his job seriously.

The ME lifted the sheet and exposed the victim's legs. "Officially, the cause of the death is blunt force trauma to the head, as I'd surmised when I first saw the body. That's not what's interesting, though. We saw evidence of bite marks at the scene, but when I removed the clothing, I found this."

Sam leaned over and peered at the body. "Both legs have bite marks in them. The new ones are bigger and deeper than what we saw Saturday. Like whatever did it worked away at the leg and tore out chunks of muscle." He lifted his gaze to stare at the doctor. "These were hidden by his jeans. That means that someone dressed him after this happened."

"Probably. I doubt he could have dressed himself." He pointed with his scalpel. "There are tooth marks on these bones, too, here, and here."

He pointed to the lower right leg. "But I was also looking at the fracture of the right tibia. I can see new bone construction. That starts forty-eight to seventy-two hours after the initial trauma. Based on gross examination, I'd say the fracture occurred two to four days prior to death."

"And the bites?"

"They are animal bites, for sure. I'd want a veterinarian to consult, but they definitely look canine to me. I thought I saw some signs of reconstruction where the teeth dug into the bone, but microscopy was inclusive."

The hair on the back of Sam's neck prickled. "You're saying he was *alive* when those bites happened?"

"I believe I said I couldn't tell." Twilling sniffed.

"Jesus." What kind of freak would let an animal gouge out chunks of muscle from a living victim? Sam controlled his breathing and tried not to think about what kind of hell this victim went through. He chewed his lower lip. "Do you have anything else?"

"Yes. The dental records you sent over were helpful. I can confirm a match. This is Mr. Eric Bell, aged nineteen. He was in remarkable shape. Or at least, he once was. He must have been an athlete." Twilling quirked an eyebrow at him. "How did you find the records so quickly?"

"I've been looking at open missing persons cases. He was wearing a letter jacket from Halsted. It was an easy guess." Sam let his gaze rest on the victim. "Eric Bell. I'll see that his parents know." Sam hated death notifications. Since Halsted was outside his jurisdiction, the sheriff's deputies would have to do it. "The body will be here?"

"Yes, but I think Social Services might want to examine it." Twilling shrugged. "Even though he's not a minor, I need to report the older fractures on this young man. His left arm has been broken at least four times, his right one twice, and there is evidence of broken ribs as well. If he were younger, I'd be obliged to report suspected child abuse." He scowled. "I don't have to call in the social workers in this case, but if his parents have other children...well, you follow my thinking."

Sam looked at Eric's body. No wonder he'd been a runaway. Some kiddos just had no luck. "How recent were these breaks?" It was always possible there was a direct line from the earlier abuse to Eric's death. Maybe there wasn't a serial killer on the loose after all.

"All but one of those appear to be more than ten years old. But one happened within the last two years."

"Poor kid. First he gets abused while he's growing up, then this happens to him."

"I didn't say he was abused. I said the law would require I file a report. In any case involving a pattern of traumatic injury to a minor, reporting is mandatory. Someone else decides if it's abuse or just bad luck. Under the circumstances, though, I think someone needs to pay a visit to his family." He reached for a bulging plastic bag. "Here are Mr. Bell's clothes and other effects. Not much, I'm afraid."

Sam accepted them. "I think I'll be there for the death notice myself. When will I have your official report?"

"I've got a few more tests to run. Now that we know who he is, I'd like to obtain his medical records for comparison. See if you can get a release from his parents."

"Either that or a subpoena, under the circumstances. Will do. Anything else?"

"No." Twilling turned away in dismissal, picked up a microphone, and started dictating notes.

"Thank you, Doctor. You've been most thorough."

Twilling scowled and shushed him.

Asshole to the end. Sam retreated to the locker room and stripped off the scrubs. His next step was to call the Sheriff and get on the death notice squad. That visit would be dicey. Were Eric's parents mourners or murderers? For sure they were suspects now, and Sam wanted to interview them.

On the way back to his car, Sam spotted a flyer from the College's theater department for a production of *Sweeney Todd.* He still needed to follow up with Allen, and dinner and a play might make a good first date. He pulled out his cell phone, but then stopped. It was only 8:30, and he had no idea what hours Allen kept. Closer to noon would be better for a call. He sent a text instead, asking if Friday night would be okay for their date.

****

Sam pulled into the Halsted 7-Eleven and settled back to wait for the deputy. The town's one-block-long business district consisted of brick structures built in the 1800's that now housed craft shops, insurance agencies, and a single restaurant advertising "Maid-Rites," whatever they were. Weathered, clapboard houses huddled on a couple of dusty side streets. The town still had a high school that looked like a WPA project from another era. Sam recalled from his file that Eric had played on the local football team.

A Sheriff's cruiser pulled up next to him, and he got out. The Deputy signaled for him to get in the front seat of his vehicle.

He settled in, and offered his hand. "Sam Sondergard. Thanks for letting me join you."

"Mark Tellefson. Nice to meet you, Sam." His eyes narrowed. "You ain't from around here, are you?"

"I grew up in LA. I came up here to get my degree at Browning and was lucky enough to get a job with HPD." Tellefson. That name was familiar.

"Figured from your accent. Born and raised right here in Halsted, myself." He flipped through papers on his clipboard. "What can you tell me about what happened to Eric? I read the report. It says here you were the investigating officer when they found his body on Saturday night?"

Strange that he'd use the victim's first name. Then Sam got it. Tellefson had filed the initial missing person's report. It had been well written. Professional, really. Not what he'd expected from a rural deputy sheriff. "An officer on a routine stop found him. The Chief called me in since I had homicide experience when I was with the LAPD."

Tellefson's eyebrows crawled up his head. "Homicide? Report don't say nothin' about that."

"I don't have the final ME's report yet, but I'm sure that will be the finding. Blunt force trauma to the head." Sam hesitated. "The body had been there for a while, and it was in pretty bad shape. If you hadn't filed a thorough missing person report, we might have had a hard time with the ID. Good work with that."

Tellefson gave him a hang-dog look and shook his head. "This is going to be hard on his poor Momma, Alma May. She's been feelin' so guilty."

That got Sam's attention. "Why guilty?"

"She caught poor Eric and another boy kissin' in his bedroom. They was buck naked and doin' who knows what. She had no idea he was homo-sexual, and she laid into him pretty hard."

"She beat him?"

Tellefson scowled at him. His tone turned scornful. "What? No, nothing like that. She yelled at him is all. Told him he couldn't live under her roof unless he agreed to forsake sin. You know, religious crap. The kid ran away, and now she's all down in the dumps about it, wantin' him back no matter what her pastor says. She calls me every week, askin' if we've made any progress findin' her son." He snorted. "She shoulda thought afore she spoke, ya ask me. Ya reap what ya sow"

Sam resolved all over again to find justice for Eric. And his mother. "Now she'll never be able take any of it back. This is going to be hard on her." Sam chose his next words with care. "You're sure she didn't beat him or anything? How about her husband?"

"She'd never beat him. Her no-good husband Harley did that plenty when Eric was little, but she sicced the Sheriff on him. Harley, he was a loser if ever there was one. After Alma May got rid of him, he held up a liquor store and got sent to the pen over at Salem. They found him in the shower with his throat cut five, ten years ago. Good riddance if ya ask me."

"In the autopsy, the ME found evidence of broken bones. One was recent, from the last twenty-four months."

"Sure. Eric broke his arm at the homecoming game last fall. He played tight end, and was right good at it, too. His momma, she'd never raise a hand against her son."

"Any brothers or sisters?"

"Nah. Alma May ain't from around here, neither. She's gonna be all alone now."

"She's going to need understanding neighbors, especially now." Sam would have to find a way to connect her with the PFLAG chapter in Hollenbeck, too. "Anything else we need to cover before we do the visit?"

"You say the body weren't found right away?"

"Looks like it was in that alley for at least three weeks."

Tellefson's mouth turned hard. "Don't need to tell poor Alma May that. She won't have to do an ID or nothing, will she?"

"No. The dental records gave us a positive ID. The ME cleaned him up, but the decomp was pretty advanced."

"Maybe we can convince her to let the state bury him."

"I'll do what I can."

Tellefson locked his gaze out the windshield. "I'll drive us there. Let me do the talkin', okay?"

"Agreed. It'll be better for her to hear it from someone she knows."

This trip was already worthwhile, even though Sam still dreaded the visit. But he was back in the same place as Saturday night. A group of young men, at least some of them gay, were missing. One of them, Eric, was dead. Murdered, actually, by some sick sadist with a vicious pet. He had to know what was going on before anyone else suffered. If Chief Hartman wanted to ignore murders of gay people, well, screw him. This was important.

His phone buzzed, and he checked the message. It was from Allen, agreeing to Friday night. Some of the tension eased out of him. Even though they'd just met, he liked Allen a lot. For sure, he didn't want to hurt his feelings. But this case was important. Maybe this wasn't the time to start a new relationship. He tucked his phone back in his pocket without answering.

He'd think about that later.

Chapter 5

Friday, October 12

Allen pulled into the parking lot of Potemkin's, the restaurant he'd picked for his date with Sam. He'd arrived fifteen minutes early, just to be safe. None of the half-dozen cars in the parking lot were a Honda, so Sam wasn't there yet.

His car coughed and shuddered when he killed the engine. It almost hadn't started this evening. He was going to have to get it fixed soon or he'd be walking to and from campus.

He wiped sweat-soaked palms on his khakis and then checked his tie in the mirror. Maybe that was too much. He loosened the knot and looked again. That was some better. At least he looked less uptight. His hair bothered him, too. His buddy Charlie from the Pride Center had convinced him this spikey do would be a guy magnet. But Charlie was a flaming queen, not the best person for fashion advice when you're dating a cop.

What to do? Wait inside, or sit in the car? Twelve minutes to go. Maybe this was a mistake. Maybe Sam wouldn't show up. After all, they'd only texted a couple of times since meeting in the Union on Monday.

A brilliant orange and red sunset silhouetted the mountains that towered west of the city. They were pretty, but sometimes they made Allen feel boxed in. Like now. God knows, he didn't miss Wisconsin, but the rolling hills around Spring Green seemed freer, gentler, than the rugged beauty of the Cascades.

Allen squirmed and blocked the sun with his hand. The day was unseasonably warm, hot even. A bead of sweat ran down his temple and tickled his jaw. Time to go inside.

He pushed the door open and paused to let his eyes adjust. Muted lighting illuminated Soviet-red walls and royal blue carpets. Portraits of Lenin and Eisenstein hung in the foyer, along with a replica of a vintage, Russian language poster for *The Battleship Potemkin.* Allen hugged himself against the sudden chill of the interior.

He tossed a grin at the hostess. "Hi, Katya. Nice dress." Despite her black, strapless evening gown, she projected an air of stark efficiency. It must be the lack of makeup and short, masculine haircut.

"Good to see you, Allen. Table for one?" She picked up a menu and tipped an expectant eyebrow at him.

"No, actually. I'll be dining with someone tonight."

Her face relaxed into a cheery smile. "Excellent. Would you like a nice, romantic booth, or is this a business meeting?"

"Uh, a booth, I guess."

"Very good. Would you like to be seated or wait?"

Decisions. Shit. Which was better? "I'll sit." *If he doesn't show up, it won't be so obvious I've been stood up.*

He followed Katya to a booth with plush, blue velvet upholstery. "I'll take care of you myself tonight, Allen. For your special dinner."

"Thank you, but that's not necessary."

"It is my pleasure. Would you like the wine list?"

Allen hesitated, then decided to splurge. "Sure." He could afford the Tvishi, and it was at least authentic. He pointed at the menu and said, "We'll have a bottle of that."

After she left, Allen used his napkin to wipe perspiration from his brow. This early, the restaurant wasn't crowded, and an elderly couple were the only other patrons in sight. The woman wore a mask attached to a green tank that rested on small cart next to their table. The poor thing must have emphysema or worse. Allen hoped Sam didn't smoke.

The wine arrived, and Katya poured a glass of the straw-colored liquid for him. He tried to stop jittering. Where was Sam? He was five minutes late. He pulled out his phone. No text. Allen began to regret splurging on an entire bottle of wine.

"Sorry I'm late."

Allen gave a little start as Sam slid into the booth opposite him. God, he was even better looking than Allen remembered. Narrow hips, broad shoulders, dark stubble on his craggy cheeks. His all-black attire gave him an added edge. Good. He wore a tie, too. Black of course. "No, I was early." Allen hoped his grin didn't look too goofy. Or needy. "Any trouble finding this place?"

"No. I just used my GPS. But I had no idea this was here. I love Russian food." He poured himself a glass of wine and took a sip. His eyes crinkled at Allen over the crystal.

"It's not really Russian, exactly. It's more Georgian."

"Even better. When I was in LA, I lived with a Russian émigré. Misha used to fix us stuff he said was Georgian."

"Then you'll like this place. Even the décor is Russian. Did you see the photos of Lenin and Eisenstein at the front?"

"I recognized Lenin, but the other guy didn't look anything like Einstein."

Allen game him an impish grin, grateful for the chance to show off. "Not Einstein, Sergei Eisenstein, the Russian film pioneer. The restaurant is named for his most famous work."

"Never heard of him. Misha would have, though. He was always dragging me to film festivals before he..." Sam hesitated. "I didn't mean to bring up Misha. Sorry. Tell me about yourself."

Allen shrugged. "Nothing much. I grew up in Wisconsin, went to a little college in Iowa, and then came here for graduate school. Never had a live-in boyfriend. If you want to talk about your ex, feel free. It won't bother me."

Sam hesitated. "Okay. He's not exactly an ex. We'd stopped at a convenience store, and he ran inside to get a soda. It was his bad luck to interrupt an armed robbery. I killed the perp who shot him, but it was too late. Misha died in my arms, there in the 7-Eleven."

Shock prickled the hairs on Allen's neck. "Oh my god, that's terrible. I'm so sorry."

"Yeah, woe is me. Look, I promise this isn't the way I usually start a date. It's just we're here, and the smell of the food reminded me of him and, well, it happened. I told you so you wouldn't think there was some big mystery I was hiding." His mouth twisted down, and he took another sip of wine. "Why don't you tell me about your research? Zoology, you said? Something to do with dogs?"

Geez, the guy's eyes looked like they were tearing up. Allen's heart went out to him. He didn't know what to do, so he babbled. "That's right. I came here to work with Dr. Sarnok. His research on the canine genome is world-class, and I was lucky enough to get a fellowship. I wish you could visit the lab. The dogs there are really special. I'm writing my dissertation on one of them, Teena. She has a vocabulary of over three thousand words."

Sam blinked, whether because of tears or surprise Allen couldn't say. "A talking dog?"

"No, no. Of course she can't *talk.* But she understands words and even grammar."

"Okay. I had visions of the Jetson's dog. What was his name? Ralph?"

"Astro. 'Rowlf' was the sound he made."

Katya returned to their table and stood, hands behind her back. "Good evening gentlemen. Have you had a chance to look at the menu?"

Sam shook his head. "No. We've been chatting away, I'm afraid." He snatched it off the table and opened it.

Katya gave them a slight bow. "Very well. I'll give you a few minutes, then."

Sam held up his hand. "Wait. Allen, I assume you're familiar with the food here?"

"Sure. Everything's good."

"Why don't you order for both of us? I'll like anything, as long as it doesn't have coconut in it."

Katya dimpled. "Coconut isn't a traditional Georgian ingredient, sir."

Allen chewed on the side of his mouth while scanning the menu. Usually his dates ordered for him, not the other way around. He hoped he'd get it right. "Let's start with *khachapuri,* of course. How's the *katmis satsivi* tonight, Katya?"

"It's what I had. The chef had it, too."

"Well, we'll have that, then." He turned to Sam. "It's grilled chicken with a walnut sauce. I think I've also tasted pomegranate seeds, cilantro, and garlic."

"Sounds wonderful."

Katya beamed at them. "Will there be anything else?"

"That's it."

Sam leaned back and looked at Allen with hooded eyes. "You were telling me about your dog, Teena."

"She's not my dog. Dr. Sarnok owns the rights to her genome, and technically she belongs to the College. But she's my research subject, and I work with her every day. She's more like my best friend." Allen stopped short. That sounded pathetic. "You must think I'm an idiot."

"Nonsense. I'm fascinated. I could swear I've known cops with vocabularies of less than three thousand words. Unless, of course, you counted profanity. I'd like to meet Teena."

"The average six-year-old has a vocabulary of 14,000 words, so in human terms Teena's not special. But she's a super-star among dogs."

Katya reappeared, carrying salads. "Courtesy of the chef, gentlemen. Enjoy." She smiled and sashayed away.

They ate their salads in silence for a few minutes. The elderly couple at the next table stood to leave, the old woman wheezing while her partner helped with her oxygen mask. She reached out with a finger and caressed his cheek. He clasped her fingers and kissed her wrist. Allen didn't want to see the tremor that harried her lips.

Sam's mouth turned down as he watched them. "That's so sad."

Allen shook his head. "I don't think so. I think it's wonderful that they have each other."

"Well, I guess it's good that she's got someone to take care of her, but what about him? All he's got is a burden."

Allen remembered Trish's words. "You don't know that. He takes care of her, sure, but you saw the way she touched him. Everyone needs someone to *care* for them. There's a difference between taking care *of* someone and caring *for* them. They care *for* each other, and it's beautiful."

Sam gave Allen an appraising look. "That's really insightful. I wasn't looking at it right. I used to smoke, and I guess I was being self-righteous, blaming her for her infirmity. But you're right. They're both lucky, and it *is* beautiful." He reached out and touched Allen's hand. "Thank you."

His touch sent goose bumps zipping up Allen's arm. This was way too serious, and he didn't know what to say. Time to babble again. "Well, don't you start smoking. My boyfriend back in Iowa smoked, and it was like kissing an ashtray." There he went, being stupid again. They'd only just held hands, sort of, and here he was talking about sex. What a doofus.

Sam chuckled. "If ever I would kiss you, it wouldn't be with ashtray breath. Ah, this must be our meals."

Allen caught the misquote from Lancelot's love song in *Camelot.* A cop who could insert references to Broadway musicals in casual conversation was beyond dreamy. Maybe he'd found his own personal Knight in Shining Armor.

Katya placed a canoe of flatbread filled with melted cheese on the table between them. "Your *khachapuri,* gentlemen."

Allen broke off a hunk of bread and used it to soak up some cheese. "Try some. It's really good."

"Misha used to fix something similar, but he used French bread."

Misha again. Time to change the subject. "So you're a cop. I used to watch *Law and Order,* but other than that, I don't have any idea what you do."

That got him a grin from Sam. "It's not nearly that interesting. Mostly it's paperwork and slogging through old records." He grimaced. "You know, I've been so wrapped up in this case I'm working that I almost cancelled our date tonight."

A frigid ball of shock chilled Allen's stomach, and his face heated.

Sam's eyes widened and he held up his hand. "Hey, I'm glad I came. Really glad. I was just afraid I was too busy at work to be fair to you. I've been obsessing over this homicide investigation. That's important, but this is more important. Getting to know *you* is more important."

I'm important to him. Don't think about it, or it'll go wrong. "Homicide? I read about that. The first in, like, twenty years in Hollenbeck, right?"

"Eighteen, to be precise. My idiot boss wanted to cover it up, call it a drug overdose. The ME is kind of a jerk, but he did the right thing. A drug overdose can't cause a hole in your skull." Sam hesitated and took a sip of wine. "It was really tough notifying the vic's mother. He was only nineteen, and he'd gone from football hero to pariah when she found out he was gay. She regrets how she treated him now, but it's too late."

That sounded familiar to Allen. "His name wasn't Eric, was it?"

Sam's eyes narrowed. "Eric Bell. Yes. Did you know him?"

Allen drew a shuddering breath. "This is awful. I kind-of-sort-of knew him. I volunteer at the Pride Center. Mark — he runs the Center — arranged for temporary housing for Eric last summer, right after his mother kicked him out. He hung around for a while after that, and then stopped coming in. He'd talked about going to Portland or San Francisco, and that's what we figured he'd done. What happened?"

"That's what I'm trying to find out. It's an open case, so I can't say too much." Sam fiddled with his dinnerware. "The Pride Center is on my list of places to visit when I get time. The chief has me loaded down with other things — reviewing cold files. Missing person cases and things like that. It's slowed down the murder investigation. Not that I have many clues."

"Well, Mark might know something. Charlie, too. He works the front desk and talks to everybody." Horror turned to anger. "Why won't they let you investigate? Is it because he was gay?"

"That might be part of it." Sam shrugged. "Mostly, the chief sees it as bad publicity. He just wants me to make it go away."

Katya arrived with their meals, and their conversation turned to other things, a pleasant dance around shared interests and enthusiasms. They both loved old Hitchcock films and musicals. Sam liked watching professional football and listening to fusion jazz. Allen couldn't stand the former, but the latter might be interesting, or at least tolerable. The Rachmaninov preludes playing on the restaurant's sound system were more to his liking. Sam found his obsession with *Star Wars* "cute." They agreed that future dates wouldn't include football or George Lucas. The good news for Allen was that there would be future dates.

****

Sam winced at every murder in *Sweeney Todd*. When the eponymous hero slit his first throat in Act I, the torture Eric Bell must have endured replayed in his imagination. When Todd and his accomplice decided to bake their victims' remains in pies, all Sam could think of were the gnaw marks on Eric's limbs.

Not the best choice for a first date. At least, not when he was in the middle of a murder investigation.

The final curtain rang down, bringing applause from the audience and relief to Sam.

As they left the theater, Allen tugged on his hand. "It's such a beautiful night. Look at that moon. Let's walk around for a while."

Sam forced a smile onto his lips. "It is nice." He let Allen lead him to the Campus Commons, where *faux*-Gothic-style red brick buildings faced onto a mini-park. Sidewalks meandered through scattered oak and pine trees and around manicured flower beds. Headlights from occasional passing cars cast shadows, but otherwise they were mostly alone.

Even Evans Hall, where Sam took his classes, huddled like a dark, abandoned cathedral.

Between his caseload and classes, how was he going to find time for Allen? He couldn't just dump him, not after tonight. He was too nice for that. Too innocent. Sam needed that...what would Misha have called it? *Insouciance.*

Allen squeezed his hand. "Penny for your thoughts."

Sam grimaced. "Sorry. Just wool gathering. Thinking about my case."

"Want to talk about it?"

More than anything. But, no, brutal reality would just ruin a fairy tale evening. "I'd rather think about something pleasant. You, for example."

Allen dimpled. "I had a wonderful time tonight."

They continued in silence, holding hands, detouring around puddles in the sidewalk. The light breeze carried the fresh scent of the shower that had come and gone while they were watching Sweeney pile up victims and Mrs. Lovett bake them into pies.

Sam forced away images of serial killers, frivolous and profane. "I'm glad you enjoyed tonight. I did, too." *Stay in the moment.*

A brief gust of wind made the trees rustle overhead and swirled the leaves on the ground, exposing a slimy wad of worms. "What the crap? Look at that." Sam wrinkled his nose, remembering the infestation in Eric's gruesome remains.

Allen said, "It's the weather. They've come out because of the rain." He knelt and probed the soil at the side of the path. A gaggle of beetles waddled away from his fingers. "See, there's a whole universe down here if you know where to look."

"It's creepy. You know beetles eat dead things." *It's just like Hollenbeck, or any place else. You poke at it, and evil comes skittering out.*

Allen stayed nonchalant and cheerful, thank god. "Good thing, too. Otherwise the dead would be piling up everywhere." Allen stood, brushed himself, and took Sam's hand again. "Let's sit for a bit. I know a place down by the pond."

Sam followed him to a secluded park bench that rested under an ancient oak tree. Ducks paddled across the little lagoon, quacking and diving for food. He plopped on a bench, and Allen cuddled next to him. Yearning tugged at Sam. He'd been alone too long.

The moonlight glimmered on the water. Allen sighed. "I'm glad you sat at my table in the Union, even if you were a table thief."

"Is that what you thought I was doing?" Sam gave in and put his arm around him. "I saw you come in and decided I wasn't going to let you get away." He ran his palm over Allen's spikey hair and let the tips tickle his skin. "Did you know you have the most beautiful eyes?"

"These beady things?"

"You have eyes that were made to be kissed." So what if it was a line from Fitzgerald? With Allen it sounded right. Sam leaned forward and kissed Allen's eyelids. When they flickered open and stared at him, his breath caught in his throat. "Even here, in the moonlight, your eyes are this incredible color. I don't know that I've seen that shade of blue before."

Allen's finger traced a line down his cheek, leaving a trail of fire behind. "You're so beautiful you scare me, you know that?" He released a shuddering sigh. "The only thing I'm afraid of is that I'll lose you, now that I've found you."

Sam pulled him close and inhaled his sweet scent. Their lips touched in a silent grace note of anticipation. "We found each other, I think," Sam whispered in his ear.

Allen pressed nearer, pulling him into an urgent embrace. Their lips touched anew, and this time a thunderclap of passion buffeted Sam's body. He twisted closer. Allen's lips opened in surrender, and Sam slipped his tongue inside. Their teeth clicked as their mouths commingled.

The kiss lasted only a moment, but it promised eternity.

Allen pulled back and gazed into his face. "Where did you learn to kiss like that?"

A smiled played with Sam's lips. "I could ask you the same thing."

Allen snuggled, his heartbeat pulsing against Sam's chest. "While you were kissing me just now, I felt as if we were the only people in the universe. Like you didn't have anything else to do." His lips touched Sam's neck, making the hair on his neck prickle and sending electricity tingling down his spine.

"I felt the same way," Sam murmured. He tipped Allen's face up for another kiss, greedy for sensation and hungry for romance.

The second kiss stretched longer than the first. Allen's hands traced languid circles on his back and sent thrills racing across his flesh. Their moans merged with the quiet splash of ducks diving and the gentle rustle of leaves blowing in the breeze.

Sam gasped, withdrew, and again touched Allen's spikey hair. "With any other guy, I'd have you off in the bushes by now. But with you, I want the first time to be special."

"I know what you mean." Allen's fingers played with Sam's earlobes and followed tendons down his neck to his collar. "I want this to be more than a one night stand, you know? It's already the best first date I've ever had."

"Me too." A grin bent Sam's mouth. "Does that mean you'll go out with me tomorrow night?"

Allen sat back and fisted him in the shoulder. "Of course, you idiot."

They strolled through the park and back to the street where they'd parked their cars. A dilapidated old van slowed as it approached them, as if cruising, and then rattled away. Even the stench of its foul, blue exhaust didn't lessen Sam's euphoria.

Chapter 6

3 AM Sunday morning, October 21

Pete jogged down the dark street, sucking icy air across his raw throat. Breath puffed from his mouth in frosty clouds, and perspiration soaked his sweat shirt. His running shoes ground against the asphalt making weary chuff, chuff, chuff sounds with each stride.

Brown crabgrass sprouted from cracks in the sidewalk. He concentrated on where to take his next step, on the pain in his legs, on his rasping throat. Anything was better than thinking about the disaster his life had become.

He stopped, panting, with his hands on his knees. This was getting him nowhere. A battered bench sat under a street light a few steps away. A bus stop, except the buses hadn't run in Hollenbeck for years. It was just like the park bench three nights ago, the one where the vice cop had first hit on him and then arrested him for public indecency.

He flopped onto the bench and lifted his sweatshirt to wipe his face. His running shorts and sweatshirt both read US Navy. He'd last worn them four nights ago while jogging with the other ROTC cadets at Browning. He may as well burn them now. For sure, his life had gone up in flames. The words of his CO still stung. *We can't kick you out for being a faggot, but public indecency is still a court martial offense.* It was resign or be booted. Either way, he'd have to pay back his scholarship and the cost of flight school last summer.

All he'd done was agree to give a cop a blow job. He didn't even really *do* anything.

It wasn't like the brass had come down on Atkins when he knocked up that sixteen year old, or Flournoy for beating up his girlfriend and sending her to the hospital. Those were Article 133 violations, too. But this wasn't about justice. It was about him being gay.

The thing was, he knew he deserved it. He hated himself for being gay.

Why couldn't he be more like the guys at the Tool Box? That cute guy with the spikey hair last Saturday didn't mind being gay. He was braver than Pete. He'd never run away from who he really was. He shivered and tried to *will* himself to stop being so negative. It didn't work.

The combination of exertion and the chilly night air made his skin clammy. His leg muscles burned, and his chest ached. *I haven't run this much since boot camp.* The cold air ate into the soft tissues of his throat and lungs. He deserved the pain.

It felt good to be alone. No one ever came here, especially this late at night. Abandoned warehouses lined one side of the street. An old cemetery hid behind a scrabble of undergrowth on the other side. An unkempt chain link fence marked the boundary between the living and the dead.

The perfect place. May as well be dead.

He rubbed his thighs. Time to run some more. Anything was better than sitting here feeling sorry for himself.

A dog nosed its way through the chain link fence, sniffing at the ground. Pete stood and stretched his calves. What a mutt. Scraggly hair, head too big, and one ear's torn in half from some old injury.

Free of the fence, the dog padded up to him and sniffed at his running shoes, whimpering. Poor thing. Pete reached out and tousled the mutt's ears.

"What's with you, fella? You got no friends either?" The dog licked his hand and wagged his tail.

Pete leaned against the bench and closed his eyes. He just wanted to be alone, but the dog was having none of it. He barked once and nuzzled his shoes again. "I got nothing for you, fella." Pete sighed. "I got nothing for nobody."

Headlights crawled down the street toward the man and the dog. Pete looked away. As the van approached, the dog became more active, running into the street, then back to Pete, tail gone insane. Pete ignored him. The van rattled past with a foul stench of exhaust. He closed his eyes in disgust.

The dog yipped again, looking first at Pete then at the van. The driver parked less than half a block away in front of a warehouse with boarded up windows. Faded paint on the side read *Klosuma's*...something. He couldn't quite make it out.

The engine sputtered to a stop and the driver's door clunked open. This was just how it had started last week, when the vice cop cruised him. Except this vehicle was a junk heap. Maybe he'd go away. Pete just wanted to be left alone.

A dirty, skinny man crawled out of the van. God, he's creepy looking. Not that it matters. Not that anything matters.

The van was parked in the shadows between yellow pools of illumination from streetlamps. The man reached in and pulled out bags of groceries. One arm was in a cast. He fumbled with them, using only the other arm.

The dog barked one more time and then scrambled to the man, who shouted, "Shoo, go away dog!"

The man's voice was feeble, whiny even. The dog sniffed all around the man's legs and feet. Now that Pete got a better look, he was bigger than he'd originally guessed.

The old fellow juggled his groceries, but then he got his feet caught up by the dog and stumbled. One of the sacks ruptured and the man teetered, losing his balance. In the next instant, he lay sprawled on the sidewalk surrounded by boxes of cereal and bags of potato chips. Canned goods rattled away down the sidewalk.

"Shee-it. Goddamn dog." His voice warbled, as if he were close to tears. His gaze landed on Pete. "Hey, mister! Could you help an old man?" Pete tried to ignore him. "Please mister. I hurt my arm again." He held up his cast. "Could you please help me?"

Pete sighed. Maybe if he helped, the man would leave him alone. He strode to where the man knelt.

"Oh, thank you, young fella. My name's Bobby."

Pete knelt and started gathering up canned goods.

"What's your name, fella?" Bobby rubbed his wrist, hacked, and spit.

"Uh, Pete." He stacked all the groceries in a heap. Now what? The paper bag was ripped and useless.

Using his good arm, Bobby tried stacking canned goods into the torn bag but they rolled again. "Thank you, Pete. You're a good person."

The man's high, bubbly voice grated on Pete's nerves. He wished he'd just shut up. "Do you maybe have another sack? That one's ruined."

Bobby clambered to his feet. "I've got something in the back of my van. Just give me a minute." The rear door creaked open and he poked around inside. "I don't know, my arm hurts bad. I think I broke it again." The dog now hunkered at Bobby's feet, his eyes never leaving Pete, his tail switching back and forth. "You're so kind to help me."

Pete finished gathering the scattered groceries. Bobby stank to high heaven, and the van was even worse. He wondered if Bobby lived in the van, or maybe he was a squatter living in one of the abandoned warehouses. The poor guy had it tough that seemed certain. Maybe Pete's life wasn't so awful after all.

Bobby hovered over him, one hand worrying the cast. "You're so kind. I wonder if you could help me? I know I got more sacks in my van. My arm hurts so bad. Could you take my bags inside for me?" Bobby's voice seemed to erupt from diseased depths inside his throat.

Pete sighed. He really did feel sorry for the old guy. "Sure, why not? I got nuthin' else to do." He stood. "Where they at?"

"Here, inside the van." The man pointed at the open rear door. "They're behind the seat. If you just crawl in you'll see them. Thanks so much, young man. You're so kind."

"Sheesh, what you been keepin' in there? Dead bodies?" Pete held his breath and crawled into the van.

The dog jumped in next to him, his tongue lolling out if his mouth and his dark eyes locked on Pete. The van swayed and a shadow blocked the light from the street. Pete turned just in time to see Bobby raise a crowbar, a gap-toothed grin on his face.

The pain only lasted for a few seconds before the world turned black.

Chapter 7

Friday, October 26

Sam stood in the dining alcove of his efficiency apartment and examined the table setting. He chewed his lower lip, moved a wine glass a few millimeters to the left, and refolded one of the napkins. It's not like things had to be perfect. He just liked it better when they were. The clock on the stove read 6:04. Where was Allen?

He returned to the kitchenette, checked the salmon steaks marinating in the refrigerator and tasted the salad dressing. A little tart. A few dribbles of honey would take care of that. The vegetables were ready to steam in the microwave, and the ganache on the cake he'd bought this afternoon at the bakery glimmered in the fluorescent lighting.

The doorbell chimed and brought a grin to his face. He called out, "Come on in. It's unlocked." Not that it mattered. They'd exchanged keys to their apartments last weekend, after their fourth date. Two weeks in, and they were already at, what? Six dates? No, seven, counting lunch at the Union this week.

Allen walked into the kitchen carrying a bottle of wine and gave Sam a hug. "Can I do something to help?"

"Sure. The veggies are in the 'fridge and the steamer's on the counter. If you could stick them in the microwave and set it for six minutes, I'll grill the salmon. Oh, and pour us some wine. What did you bring?"

"Just a cheap Reisling."

"Perfect with fish." Sam tested the skillet with a bead of water. Not quite ready. "How was your day?"

Allen rolled his eyes. "Don't ask. I'll tell you later. How about yours?"

"Same old, same old." There. It was hot enough now. The pink fish sizzled in the skillet while Sam dusted it with sesame seeds. "Still no leads on the Eric Bell case. The Chief won't let me spend any time on it. He wants me to close it out as unsolved. There's some ROTC cadet that's missing, and he wants me to work on that instead. Seems his parents are politically connected."

Allen poured a glass of wine and set it on the counter next to Sam. "What are you going to do?"

"Well, there's something up with the cadet, that's for sure. He resigned his commission for no apparent reason a couple weeks ago, and then just disappeared. The other cadets aren't talking, and there's a wall of silence from the Navy staff. The chief is right. This case deserves someone's attention. But I've got a murder to investigate, damn it. That's got to be more important."

"Yeah. I wish I could help. I did ask at the Pride Center, and no one had heard from Eric in months."

"Thanks for that. I should have gone there myself, but the Chief's watching me like a hawk. He won't let me work the case when I'm on the clock. Off the clock, I've been a little busy. In case you hadn't noticed." He flipped the salmon. "Another two or three minutes. There's salad in the 'fridge, too. Can you get it out?"

Allen stood in place and gave him an impish grin. "Yes, I can do that."

Sam frowned then got it. "Okay, since we've established you've got the *ability* to get it out, *will* you please get it out?"

"Sure thing." Allen opened the door and pulled out a bowl.

Sometimes Allen's sense of humor was funnier than other times. Sam nodded to the refrigerator. "That cup next to it has the dressing. Give it a swish with the whisk and drizzle it on, if you don't mind. Dinner's almost ready."

Allen placed the salad on the table, returned to the kitchen and gave Sam a kiss on his cheek. "You're so efficient. Look at this place. Where are the dirty dishes?"

"In the dishwasher, of course. I clean as I go." Another minute.

"I hope that's not a criticism of my culinary technique."

Sam bit his lower lip and didn't answer. He'd spent thirty minutes cleaning up Allen's kitchen after dinner two weeks ago. "Not at all. But I don't have a roommate, so it's easier for us to get together here." He drizzled sauce onto the dinner plates he'd set by the stove and then placed the salmon on them. The microwave dinged. "Perfect timing." In another few seconds, he carried the plates into the dinette. "Time to eat."

Allen followed him and paused before sitting. "Wow. Look at this. Cloth napkins folded to look like hats, dishes that match each other, and chives scattered over the salmon. Not to mention that the sauce looks like Jackson Pollock painted it on the plates. Fancy."

Sam's face heated. "Thanks, but it's all quick and easy. I couldn't do anything in the kitchen if it weren't for Rachel Ray. The garnish and sauce just make it look hard." He gestured to the table. "Sit."

Allen held up a finger. "Wait. I know all you've got is that fusion jazz stuff."

"I thought you liked Nora Jones."

"I do, but I brought some classic rock. For variety." He pulled a CD from his pocket. "Do you mind if I stick this in your stereo?"

"No problem." Sam gave a little start and realized he'd forgotten to light the candles. By the time they sat down to eat, the dinette had been transformed into an intimate nook. The rest of the apartment disappeared in the shadows cast by the flickering flames. Moody Blues singing "Nights in White Satin" oozed from the sound system.

Allen took a tentative bite of the salmon, and his face lit up. "This is awesome."

Satisfaction welled in Sam. "All due to Rachel Ray and the Food Network, believe me." He had to admit it wasn't bad. He held up his wine glass. "A toast."

Allen raised his. "To us."

"I was going to toast Rachel, but yours is better." Their glasses clinked together.

They ate in silence for a few minutes before Sam asked, "So, are you ready to tell me about your day?"

Allen rolled his eyes. "I guess, but it seems a shame to let that asshole Sarnok ruin this great dinner."

"He's on a roll, again, then?"

"Is he ever. I think the Army's putting pressure on him. All the bigwigs are scheduled to go to Fort Huachuca in Arizona on Monday."

"Huachuca? Isn't that where the Army Intelligence School is at?"

"I guess. As near as I can tell, Army Intelligence has the same relation to intelligence as Army music has to music."

"That would be none, I assume?"

"You got that. Sarnok's been really pressing me for results. Working poor Teena like a dog."

"Well, she is a dog." Sam grinned. Allen was so cute when he got worked up.

"You know what I mean. Sarnok's hot for a real-world test, and she's not ready."

"I know you've run her through simulated search-and-rescue scenarios. What's wrong with a real world test?"

"Our test environment is controlled, with minimal distractions. She does fine there, but there's no telling what would happen if she ran free in the streets."

"You're worried she might get run over by a car or something?"

"There's that, but she's so trusting. She might follow the orders of the bad guys, for example, or just random strangers. Or another dog might distract her. They might even mate. That would be a disaster."

Sam kept his mouth still and didn't laugh. Allen was worried about his pet being raped? He was so geeky, sometimes. That just made him more adorable. "I know how much you care for her."

"It's not that. I mean, I do. But we can't let her genotype out in the wild. The early generations, before number six, all were unstable. Hostile. Vicious, even."

"Like pit bulls?"

"Pit bulls have to be trained to be violent, but, yes, like that. Except those dogs couldn't be domesticated. Too much non-canine DNA in them."

"Non-canine DNA? I've heard about intermixing species with crops, but not with animals." That was really creepy sounding.

"Researchers have been doing it for years. They've injected spider genes into goats, and their milk produced fibers for bullet-proof vests. That's just one example."

"So, Teena has spider DNA?" Sam frowned. Allen was a sweetheart, but he could be hard to follow sometimes. "Maybe that would account for her Spidey sense."

Allen's mouth turned down. "Ha ha. Very funny. The Army classified those details. I can't tell you what DNA Sarnok used."

"But you're worried. If she's not ready, she's not ready. What are you going to do?"

Allen slumped and toyed with his salad. "I don't know. I've talked to the project veterinarian, Dr. Harzik. He agrees with me. Maybe he can do something."

Sam frowned at the mention of Harzik. The ME never did find a veterinarian to consult on those bite marks on Eric's legs. Maybe there was a clue there. "I wish I could help. In fact, I'd like to talk to this Harzik guy. The ME needs to consult with a veterinarian on, uh, a case we're working. Your veterinarian might be helpful to both of us."

Allen gave him a forlorn look. "Harzik's an okay guy. A little creepy, though. It feels sometimes like he's hitting on me. He looks kind of like an aging Jerry Garcia. I'm sure he'd be willing help both of us if he could." A half-hearted smile bent his features. "I'll ask him to join us for lunch next week in the cafeteria, if you want."

"That'd be perfect." Time to turn this conversation to something lighter. "You want dessert now or later?"

"It looks fantastic, but later sounds better. This was a really good meal." He stood. "I'll help clean up, and then maybe we can watch a movie. I put *Shadow of a Doubt* in my queue."

"Hitchcock, right?" Sam joined him in gathering up dishes.

"Yeah. Thornton Wilder wrote the screen play. It's about a serial killer in small-town USA. I thought it would be right up your alley."

Something lighter would have been better, but Sam just nodded. "Sounds interesting."

They cuddled together on the sofa as the opening credits rolled across the screen. Sam squeezed Allen's shoulder. "You're staying the night, right?"

"If you'll have me." Allen squirmed closer and kissed him on the lips. "I might have to in any case. My car almost didn't start. It's too far to walk."

"You shouldn't walk around that neighborhood where you live. It's only half a mile from where we found Eric."

"Hey, my roommate walks to and from campus all the time. That's one of the reasons I rented there. That and it's cheap."

"Just be careful." Sam's phone buzzed. "Damn it. I'm supposed to be off duty tonight."

Allen nuzzled his neck. "Just let it ring. I've got plans for you tonight."

"Can't. They wouldn't call unless it was an emergency." Or whatever the chief decided was an emergency. He pulled his phone from his shirt pocket and punched the screen. "Sondergard here."

"Sam, this is Karen. We've got a real situation developing."

He stood and headed to the bedroom where he kept his ready kit. "Talk to me."

"One of the professors at Browning found a human hand at her research habitat. A squirrel farm, if you can believe that."

"A hand? You mean, like a disarticulated hand? Just laying around?"

"Disarticulated, yes. But it had been buried. This professor was digging around and found it.

"She was digging? Why?" Sounded suspicious to Sam.

"For squirrel shit for all I know. Ask her. They've got her at the scene. The ME and a couple of officers are there too, and they've found more body parts. ME says he's never seen anything like it. The Chief's even headed out there."

Holy shit. That wasn't good. Not good at all. No telling how he'd muck things up. "Shit. How many bodies?" He clipped his service revolver to his belt and shrugged into his Kevlar vest. "How long have they been there?"

"ME says one is fresh, and the other for months. He thinks at least two bodies, maybe more. Just a second." Sam took advantage of the silence to slip into his black hiking boots. Allen, wide-eyed, leaned in the door frame, watching.

Karen spoke again from the phone. "That was the Chief. He wants you on the site with him as soon as possible. You're the closest we've got to a forensic expert, Sam."

"Damn it, I can't do this by myself. He needs to call in the state police. They'll have a proper team in place."

"Like that's going to happen. Hurry, Sam. He's on a tear. You ready for the address?"

Sam opened his notebook and picked up a pen. "Go." He copied the address and read it back to her. "I'm not sure where that's at."

"East side of town, in the Oak Crest addition."

"Got it. Tell him I'll be there in, say, twenty minutes. Sondergard out." He broke the connection and turned his gaze to Allen. "Sorry. I gotta go. Some professor at the University found a bunch of bodies at a squirrel farm, if you can believe it."

"Squirrel farm? You mean Dr. Eckhorn? I know her! Is she all right?"

"Don't know. Probably, or they would have said something. Freaked, I bet. It can't be every day you go digging for squirrel droppings and find human body parts. It sounds like someone's used it as a body dump." Sam thought about all those unsolved missing person cases. Sweet Jesus, what if they led to this? "Where's my jacket?"

"In the closet. I'll get it." Allen handed it to Sam, his hands trembling. "Shit. I did field work at her habitat last year, for her class. A body dump?"

"Yeah. I'm the only one on the force with any real forensic experience. I'm going to have to be the lead on this." He hung his badge on a leather strap about his neck. "I'm really sorry, babe, but I have to go. I don't know when I'll be back."

Allen gazed at him with sober eyes. "Will you be okay?"

Sam heaved a deep breath and peered at his lover. "Sorry, you're new to this. This is part of being with a cop. Yeah, I'll be safe. The bodies have been there a while, so there's no danger tonight. Besides, there's always backup, and I wear a Kevlar vest when I'm on duty. You've seen my gun." Allen grinned at that, and he smiled back. "I mean the other one, the one that shoots bullets. But look, this is going take over my life for a while. I'm afraid I won't be much company." He quirked an eyebrow at Allen. "Forgive me?"

"Sure. Of course. Just be careful. I don't want to lose you. I just *found* you."

"Don't worry, babe. You're stuck with me. Stay here as long as you like. You've got your keys. I've got to rush." He gripped Allen by the shoulders. "Give me one last kiss." He gave Allen a quick peck on the cheek and dashed out the door.

Chapter 8

Friday, October 26

Sam gripped the steering wheel, leaned forward, and peered into the darkness. Drizzle fell from overcast skies, and a chilly wind buffeted his car. The suspension creaked as the vehicle lurched through a pothole, sending muddy rainwater cascading across his windshield. His wipers swooshed it away in grimy streaks.

He glanced at his GPS. Almost there. Houses, a quarter of them boarded up and with unkempt lawns, crammed close together in yesterday's dream of suburban bliss. Cracked sidewalks, broken streetlights, and crumbling roads spoke of today's reality.

He rounded a corner. The swirling lights of four police cruisers turned the raindrops into blood-red beads that streamed across the safety glass. The Chief and the ME stood under an umbrella outside an open gate. Someone had stretched yellow crime scene tape between the posts, but now it lay in a trampled mess in the mud. Beyond, flashlights held by invisible hands floated through scrabbled woodland. Sam squinted through the murk and read the bright red lettering on the sign chained to the gate.

Browning State College
NO TRESPASSING
Department of Zoology
S. Beecheyi Habitat

He stepped out of his car. He considered getting his plastic poncho from the trunk, but the Chief waved him to approach.

"About time you got here, boy." The Chief glared at him, his eyes ruddy and reptilian in the reflected light from the cruisers. "I'm puttin' you in charge, what with your big city experience. You seen shit like this all the time in LA, I bet. Now get crackin', you hear? We got to look like we're doin' something besides standin' around with our thumbs up our butts. "

Sam had his own ideas what was up the Chief's butt, but instead kept his gaze on the habitat. At least the Chief wasn't trying to cover things up and pretend like nothing happened like he did with the Bell case. That was progress. He nodded to the flashlights. "What's going on out there?"

The ME's mouth formed a grim line, and his voice was flat. "The Chief has officers digging up the crime scene, looking for more body parts. They've already found parts of at least three different individuals."

Digging up the crime scene. Great. So much for a professional investigation. Sam swiped rain off his scalp. Three bodies. Three *more* bodies, in addition to Eric Bell's. "That's four murders in Hollenbeck this month."

A voice called from inside the habitat. "We've got another one, Doc."

The ME closed his eyes, and his jaw muscles jumped. "I'll be right there." He picked up a body bag and stalked off into the woods.

Sam had to at least try to insert some professionalism into the investigation. "Chief, we shouldn't be doing this. We need a professional team in there to process this scene. Our police aren't trained for anything this complex. They're going to destroy whatever evidence is out there."

His boss pinched his mouth together and scowled at him. "You sayin' our boys is incompetent? We ain't going to have no outsiders here. No state po-lice, and for sure no Feebs. I told you that before."

"But — "

The Chief grabbed him by his jacket and pulled him close. "Now you listen to me, Mr. Big City Cop. We handle our own problems. There ain't gonna be no more talk about callin' in outsiders." He released Sam with a push. "I hired you because you're supposed to be able to handle shit like this. You'll do what I tell you. You got that, boy?"

Sam thought about talking to the DA, but he was another political crony of the mayor and the Chief. The ME returned and handed a limp body bag to the waiting EMT, who dumped it into a pile in her ambulance. Whatever it contained, it couldn't have been a whole corpse. Sam scowled. They weren't even attending to the chain of evidence.

"I asked you a question, boy." The Chief snarled.

Sam kept his face expressionless and re-ran the Chief's last words in head. Ignoring the 'boy,' he was telling him to obey orders. "I got that, sir." He surveyed the scene again. "Who first found the parts?"

"Some fruitcake professor. She went all bananas."

"Well, I should interview her. Where is she?"

The Chief shrugged. "She's in one of the patrol cars." He pointed. "We already done talked to her. You should be lookin' for clues with the rest of my men."

Sam's throat tightened, and his face heated. "Sir, did you not put me in charge of this investigation?"

"I said so, didn't I? But you're under my direction, boy. Don't you forget that. Don't think you can go callin' in no outsiders."

"Yes, sir. If I'm in charge, I need to interview the only witness we've got."

A van with the letters KPTV on the side pulled into the street and stopped behind Sam's Honda. The Chief's eyes lit up. "Well, lookee there. All the way from Portland, right here in Hollenbeck." He turned to Sam. "Talk to whoever you want. Just you make sure I get twice daily reports, in writing, starting first thing in the morning. I'll handle the press." He pulled his belt up over his belly and swaggered toward the TV crew that emerged from the van.

"God help us," Sam muttered.

The ME grunted. "He's an ass, all right. I play poker with the DA. Maybe I can talk some sense into him."

A pleasant shock of surprise lifted Sam's eyebrows. "You think?" At least the ME was smart, even if he could be a jerk.

The physician snorted. "Probably not. He's just another political hack. Tell you what. They can't stop me from calling in the State Medical Examiner. We'll at least get a real forensics report on the body parts. Don't expect much, though. The decomp's pretty advanced."

"Thanks. Any idea who took first report? I need a proper briefing."

"None. Dispatch called me, and the place was already crawling with cops with the Chief shouting orders when I got here. Between the rain and their thumb-fingered digging, there's not likely to be much useful evidence left."

"I guess I can call dispatch and find out." Sam slid into the nearest cruiser and used the radio. "Karen, who took the initial call on the Oak Crest incident?"

"You mean the squirrel farm? Bateman."

"Is he still on duty? Can you buzz him on his shoulder mike? I'm outside the crime scene, and I need briefed by someone besides the Chief."

"Sure. Just a second." Moments later she came back on. "He's headed your way. Otis Bateman."

"Thanks. Sondergard out."

Sam stood in the rain next to the cruiser and waited. A middle-aged officer, muddy and rain-soaked, trudged through the gate and approached him. "You Detective Sondergard?" He stuck out his hand. "Otis Bateman, here."

"I'm Sam. Nice to meet you. Let's get out of this rain." He gestured to the cruiser he'd just used.

Otis squeezed his features. "Jesus, I could really use a cigarette. Can we find a tree or something to stand under instead? Would you mind?"

"Sure." They walked to an oak standing just outside the habitat's fence. It still had most of its leaves, but each gust of wind sent a few more spiraling to the ground. Sam shivered and said, "What a mess."

Otis's face glowed red as he lit a cigarette. He exhaled a cloud of smoke and sighed. "You can say that again." He offered the pack to Sam.

He chewed on his cheek. Back in LA, cigarettes had lubricated his work. They eased tension and filled boring interludes. They were an essential part of the groove of his investigative routine. "No thanks. I quit."

"Good for you." Otis inhaled again and coughed. "The Chief's got us bumbling around the crime scene, screwing things up. We should have the state police here, helping." He sighed. "It wasn't always like this. The old chief was a good man. Professional."

Nice to know at least some of his fellow officers shared his view of the leadership. "Well, we've got the leaders we've got. What can you tell me? I understand you took the initial report."

"Yeah. It was from the neighbors. They heard someone screaming. When I came to investigate, I found the gate open and that Browning State jeep parked over there. I followed my ears and found this hysterical woman, shrieking her head off."

"I understand she'd found a disarticulated hand."

"Yeah, but it took a while to get that out of her. She kept raving about her squirrels."

"Squirrels?"

"Yeah. I guess she studies them or something. She's a professor at the college." He pulled his notebook from an interior pocket in his jacket. "Lucy Eckhorn. She rattled on about the damned squirrels like some folks do about their kids. I swear, she was more upset about us disturbing her beloved little pests than finding a dismembered body."

Sam blinked and dead-panned, "So you're saying she's kind of squirrelly."

That got him a combination laugh and snort from Otis. "You got that right." The man descended into a fit of coughing.

Sam waited until Otis hacked and spit, and then asked, "You think she has anything to do with the deaths?"

"You mean other than finding the hand? Nah." He snuffed his cigarette against his boot, field stripped it, and put the butt in his pocket. "But I'll tell you what. Something is going on here. Something evil."

"Where's this Eckhorn woman? I'd like to talk to her."

"Good luck with that. She's nuts, if you ask me." He pointed. "She's in the back of my cruiser. The Chief wouldn't let me send her home."

"Thanks, Otis. You can take a break if you want."

"Thanks, but now that I've had a smoke I'll go back. Who knows, maybe I'll find something." He straightened his back and splashed through the mud back into the habitat.

Sam trotted through the rain and slid into the rear seat of the cruiser where Dr. Eckhorn sat. The windows were fogged over, but a ruddy glow from the other cruisers bathed the interior in strobes of light and darkness.

A bedraggled woman huddled next to him, clutching a gray police blanket. She stared at him with puffy, red-rimmed eyes that looked through him instead of at him. Gray hairs straggled in a wet tangle from the bun unraveling at the back of her neck.

"Good evening, ma'am. I'm Detective Sam Sondergard. You're Dr. Eckhorn?"

She nodded.

"I wonder if I might ask you a few questions?" He opened his notebook.

She wiped at her eyes, streaking mud on her face. "Can't you make them stop, officer?" Her voice trembled, and tears leaked down her cheeks.

"I'm a detective, ma'am." *Why did civilians always get that wrong?* He played her question back in his mind. "Uh, make who stop?"

"Those men! They're destroying my habitat! Look at them, traipsing around, digging, destroying! What will my *spermophilus beecheyi* do?"

"Spermi-what, ma'am?" *Otis was right. She's nuts.*

Tears didn't stop her eyes from rolling or her voice from cutting like a saber. "*Spermophilus beecheyi.* I suppose *you'd* call them ground squirrels, like those awful people in the neighborhood. But this is *my* research habitat, and *their* home! And now all those awful men are out there with shovels, digging it up. Destroying it. Can't you do something?"

"Ma'am, didn't you find a disarticulated human hand there today?"

"Yes, surely. That was awful too. It was all covered with ants. Right there with my poor, innocent *S. Beecheyi.* And now *they're* being punished instead of the criminals! That's just like you cops!"

Sam got it. She thought *squirrels* were more important than his murder victims. "Ma'am, we have to investigate. They've found pieces of at least three bodies out there. Maybe four." He tapped on his notebook with his pen. "For starters, why don't you tell me about this habitat. You use it for research? Just tell me who comes here, what it's for, and so on. Then I'll see what we can do."

She tugged at a tangle of hair and settled into her seat. "I'll have you know, officer, that I've run this habitat since I came to Browning College thirty years ago. It was ideal, back then. Out in the country, teaming with *S. Beecheyi.*" Her voice dropped to a conspiratorial whisper. "I've presented papers to the State Zoological Society on them, you know. They've been nominated for awards."

"Yes, ma'am. I got that you study these, uh, ground squirrels." Typical researcher. Nothing mattered but her peculiar obsession. Just like Professor Mondrian. Her lectures always meandered off into digital forensics no matter what the subject. Keep her focused that was the trick. "Tell me, who, besides yourself, comes here?"

"Well, students in my field zoology classes. But I haven't taught that for over a year."

"So you're the only person who's been here for the last year, ma'am?"

"I didn't say *that*, officer. Really, I'd think you could listen better!"

Officer again. He wasn't one of her squirrels, so details like his title didn't matter to her. "So who else comes here ma'am?" Patience.

"Those awful neighborhood children, for one. They think my habitat is a park, to play in. And their older siblings are worse, degenerate. I swear I found *beer cans* and *condoms* in here last summer. I'd think you'd know. I filed a trespass complaint with you people."

Like the police had nothing better to do that enforce trespass orders. "Yes, ma'am. We'll check that out. Do you have any names of people we should talk to?"

"Hardly. You people never would do anything about my complaint. But there's the parents. You might talk to them. They sued to have my habitat closed. They called it a nuisance. They said my *S. Beecheyi* were digging up their lawns, ruining their property values. As if their lawns were more important than science."

This wasn't getting him anyplace. "Ma'am, I wonder if you could just tell me what happened today? What you were doing and what you found?"

"Well, I was here gathering data. Did you know that spermophilus beecheyi have the most *interesting* mating habits? They — "

Sam held up his hand, palm forward. "Ma'am, please. Just tell me what happened today."

She sniffed. "Well. I saw that the ground was disturbed, like someone had been digging. Last summer I found possum traps in my habitat. I'm sure that the neighbors set them. Can't you investigate that, officer?"

"I'm a homicide detective, ma'am, but I'll be sure to pass that on to the right people. Go on, please. Tell me what happened."

"Well, I saw the ground was disturbed, so I got down on my knees and dug, with my hands, you know? Sure enough, I found blood and this *thing* down there. I thought it was one of my *S. Beecheyi*, but instead it was a hand. It was dreadful. That was when I called the police."

According to Otis, the neighbors had actually called, but he didn't challenge her version. "So you found this hand. Have you ever found anything like that before here?"

"I told you. They killed one of my *S. Beecheyi* last month."

Squirrels again. Of course. "But you hadn't found any *human* parts before."

"Don't be silly. I would have reported it." She sniffed again.

"How about people loitering here, people who shouldn't be here? Have you seen that?"

Lucy's face flushed. "Yes! Weren't you listening? Those loutish neighbors, their bratty kids, and their degenerate teenagers!"

A hand rapped on the door and Sam swiped at the window. Otis was back, holding a plastic evidence bag.

Sam turned back to Dr. Eckhorn and closed his notebook. "Well, thank you ma'am. We'll probably have some more questions for you, later." He paused. "Would you like a ride someplace? There's no reason for you to stay here."

"No. I have to stay. I have to watch." Lucy again rubbed her sleeve against the fog on the window and stared outside.

Sam stepped back into the rain and asked Otis, "What you got?"

"Another disembodied hand. But this was buried with it." He dangled the baggy, which held a crumpled a micro SD card. "I took photographs with my cell phone to document where we found it. After the ME took the hand away, I bagged it for evidence."

"Good work." Something useful at last.

"Yeah. I thought it might be from a camera, or maybe a cell phone. But it's all bent out of shape and soaked in mud and who knows what else."

Sam peered at it and thought of Professor Mondrian and her peculiar obsession. This was just down her alley. "Log it in, will you? I think I know just the person for this. If anyone can pull data from it, she can."

Otis nodded. "I hope so." A voice called from the habitat, drawing his gaze. "It's pretty bad out there. Whoever did this is a real bad guy. We've all got your back, Detective."

The Chief's voice bellowed from across the parking area, where he and the ME huddled under an umbrella. "Sondergard. Come over here."

Sam gave Otis a curt nod. "Thanks. That's good to know. You've done good work tonight." He trotted through the rain to answer his summons.

The Chief nodded toward the figure in the car. "Learn anything from the whack job professor?"

"It's been pretty hard on her, sir. Finding a body like that, and now we're digging up her life's work. She's pretty upset." *Asshole. You could show her some respect.*

The Chief snorted. "She'll get over it. Just some egghead." He surveyed the scene. "Well, boy, it sure looks like you've got your work cut out." He glared at Sam. "You know this'll take a lot of time. You'll probably hafta quit school until this case is solved."

That needled Sam in exactly the wrong place. Sure, he'd already thought about dropping out to investigate the Bell murder. But the Chief didn't have any frigging business telling him not to go to school. "Sir, you know that I attend classes in my off-hours."

"That was before this came up, Detective. You're to think about nothing else but this case until you've got it wrapped up. No classes. No social life. This *case* is your life, as of right now. You hear me?"

Sam made no comment. An image of Allen as he had left him earlier tonight, alone in his apartment, flashed across his memory. No blubbery, fat-ass, stupid small-town politician was going to tell Sam how to handle his social life. *Where's the union when you need it?*

He took a deep breath to steady himself. Just because the Chief was a boorish asshole didn't mean he wasn't right. This case was important, maybe the most important of his career. For sure it was important to victims and their families. He wondered how many of these bodies would match up with his missing person cases.

"I asked you a question, Mister." The chief growled.

"Yes sir. I hear you." He was going to solve these murders no matter what. Not because the Chief told him to, but despite the Chief and his obstruction.

He pulled his leather jacket tighter against the rain and the cold fall air. The crew continued to dig, the rain continued to fall, and the lights on the police cruisers continued to flash. Lucy Eckhorn huddled in the Chief's patrol car, weeping.

Sam gritted his teeth and re-read the sign outside the habitat. Maybe there was a way to call in help, after all. He knew what he had to do Monday morning, first thing.

Chapter 9

Monday, October 29

Sam bounded up the stairs of the criminology building. A mob of freshmen headed to their 9:30 classes, leaving muddy trails on the drab, terrazzo floors of the mid-century modern structure. He clutched a leather briefcase in one hand and used the other to balance a cardboard tray holding two coffees. He stopped outside an open office door and peeked inside. "Dr. Mondrian? Are you here?"

"That you, Sam?" Despite her five-foot-one frame, her voice was a lusty contralto. "Come on in."

He used his foot to push the door open and looked for a place to set the tray.

A wide grin split her face. "You brought coffee. Bless your heart." She stood and swept a stack of ungraded essays to one side.

Sam deposited the tray in the cleared space and settled into the guest chair — the one that didn't contain a crooked stack of books. "I've got cream and sugar in my briefcase if you need it."

She popped the plastic lid off one cup and blew on it. Steam fogged her wire-frame glasses. "I like it black, thanks." She leaned back in her chair and stared at him. "I saw the news. Pretty awful. Are you involved with the case? Is that what you needed to see me about?"

Sunlight shone through the windows behind her, changing her perfectly coifed curls into a golden halo. If Sam hadn't known better, he'd have thought she was the trophy wife of some rich dude instead of a world-class forensic scientist. How does she manage to look like that and still be a professor? She must have her own personal style elf living in her closet, picking out what to wear and advising on makeup. If so, she could use an office elf, too, to clean up this mess.

Focus. He squinted against the glare. "I'm the lead investigator. And yes, that's why I emailed you yesterday. I could use your assistance on a couple of things."

"Glad to help." She rose to close the blinds. "Sorry. I didn't really mean to be like Charles Laughton in *Witness for the Prosecution.*" When she was seated again, she continued, "It won't be the first time I've consulted with law enforcement. It'll be the first time that idiot Hartman has called me in, though. I'm not sure he can even spell forensic."

"The Chief doesn't know I'm here." Sam opened his briefcase and pulled out the evidence bag containing the micro SD card Otis had found. "We dug this up at the body dump, next to a disarticulated hand." He slipped one of the photos Otis had taken across the desk, showing the card in the palm of a disarticulated hand.

She picked it up and examined it. "Gruesome." She handed it back to him and eyed the baggie. "I bet you want me to pull data off that."

"I was hoping."

"May I see?"

Sam handed it to her.

She held the bag by the corner, between thumb and forefinger, as if it contained a priceless artifact. Sunlight glittered on the gold connectors as it twisted in her grip. Her eyes sparkled, and her face glowed with interest. "It's pretty screwed up. It won't fit in a card reader."

"Probably not." Disappointment dragged at Sam. Maybe she couldn't help after all.

"I'll have to hook it up manually. That'll take longer. The physical damage may have disordered the file structure, too." She moved a pile of unopened mail and deposited the bag on her desk. "I've pulled data from worse. Give me a couple of days, and I might have something for you. Or not. Too early to tell."

"At least it's not hopeless." Sam pulled paperwork from his briefcase. "You'll need to sign a consultant's agreement and fill out some documents to establish the chain of custody." He paused. "I don't want to talk to the Chief about this, so I can't offer you any payment."

She beamed at him. "You kidding? I'd pay you to do this. I live to solve these kinds of puzzles."

This was working out even better than he'd hoped. Minutes later the forms were signed, and she stood. "I think I'll have my graduate assistant take my classes today. I want to get started on this."

Sam held up his hand. "I've got one more thing to ask you about."

"You found more tech at the site?" Her eyebrows crawled up her forehead.

"No, this is more of a jurisdictional question."

"You think you don't have authority to investigate or something? That'd be Zimmer's area, not mine."

Zimmer would tie him up in endless precedents and legalisms. That wasn't what he needed. "Not exactly. Look, you know where we found these bodies?"

"Out in the Oak Crest addition." Her face lit up. "Oh, I get it. You found them on a habitat the zoology department owns. That makes the site state property, so the *state* has jurisdiction."

He knew she'd get it. "Exactly. Except the college has its own security force, so technically *they* have jurisdiction. But they could call in the state police for help if they wanted."

"Surely. But our security force just handles parking tickets and keeps the buildings locked up at night. You don't *want* them asserting jurisdiction, do you? They'd turn the whole thing over to the state police. You'd be left out in the cold."

"No. But I need the resources the state police can bring to bear. A real forensic team for example. I mean, the Chief has me storing the evidence in a garage used by the *Parks Department*, for god's sake."

She sat back down and steepled her fingers. "So what's your plan?"

"What I'd like is for the college to ask for *joint* jurisdiction with the city. After all, it looks like the murders took place somewhere else and the bodies were dumped at the squirrel farm. That keeps me on the case, but lets the college call in the additional resources we need."

"Clever. But that's going to be tricky." She frowned and drummed scarlet-tipped fingernails on her desk. "The criminology department has a good relationship with the campus security force. I could call in some chips. Chief Watson's old school, but I think I can get him to play ball. Give me a couple of days, and I can probably set this up for you."

Relief flooded through him. "You'll do that?" This was working out better than he'd ever hoped.

"No guarantees, but I'll do my best. You know our President's a political hack from the same party as the mayor and the chief of police. I think he wants to run for governor again. If he gets involved, all bets are off."

"Well, I can't be any worse off than I am now. Thank you, Dr. Mondrian."

"Jill. If we're going to be working together, call me by my first name." She picked up the evidence bag and scrutinized the SD card. "Anything else?"

"That's it. You don't know how much I appreciate this. Thank you." Sam stood, but she wasn't looking at him. Her attention was all on the SD chip. Professors and their obsessions. Just like Allen with his dogs.

Sam glanced at his watch. Time to get back to the Parks Department and continue sifting through the buckets of evidence he'd accumulated at the habitat yesterday.

On the way to his car, he pulled out his phone and called Allen. "Hey, babe. How are you?"

"Missing you. I'm getting ready for some test runs with Teena. I got loaded with a big research assignment this morning in class, too."

"You were asleep when I got in last night, and I left early this morning before you woke. But it was great having you there. I did kiss you goodbye."

"Well, there's that. *Stop that, Teena.*" Woofing sounds barked from the receiver.

Sam grinned. "I just wanted to hear your voice. I should be home tonight by seven or so if you want to come over."

"Okay. Not sure I can, though. I went to my place this morning to pick up my books, but then my car wouldn't start. I had to walk to campus, and I was late. Sarnok had a hissy fit."

Sam squeezed his mouth and frowned. "I wish you wouldn't do that. Walk to campus, I mean. I worry about you." *Damn it, there's a serial killer out there. What's he thinking?*

"I do it all the time. My roommate doesn't even own a car. I'll be fine. Really." More barks. "I should go. Talk tonight?"

"Sure." He was probably being over-protective. Misha always hated it when he did that. But then, look what had happened to him. Sam forced cheeriness into his voice. "Just be careful. Call me if you need a ride." He licked his lips. "I love you, babe." Shock at what he'd just said made him halt in the middle of the sidewalk. Where did *that* come from?

Doggie voices barked from the phone. "*Teena!* I said *stop* that. Sorry, I didn't catch the last. What did you say?"

He needed time to process what had just popped out of his mouth. Best to pretend it never happened. "I said it's not safe to walk. If you need a ride, call me."

"I'll be fine, really." More frantic doggie sounds. "I swear, sometimes she's like a two year old. Sorry. I got to go. Bye."

Sam stuck his phone back in his pocket and continued on to his car, scarcely noticing the freshmen jostling past him. He'd only known Allen a couple of weeks, but he couldn't deny there was something deep going on between them. Maybe he really was falling in love.

Right now, though, he had his case to think about.

****

After a day of sifting through buckets of dirt from the body dump, Sam stretched weary shoulder muscles and examined the pitiable piles of evidence they'd acquired. A few bones that probably belonged to squirrels, some scraps of paper, a discarded and empty pack of cigarettes. The only possibly useful item was a faded, red plastic tag that his partner Otis had exposed mid-afternoon.

Another dozen unprocessed buckets sat next to bags of fertilizer in one corner of the garage, behind the Parks Department snowplow. Chemical smells mixed with the odors of earth and decaying vegetation from the evidence buckets. "What do you think, Otis?"

The other officer stopped shaking dirt through a screen and wiped sweat from his brow, leaving a streak of red dirt behind. He lit a cigarette, inhaled, and his features relaxed. "We got a couple of good leads, Sam. Them bones is probably just squirrels, but there's that tag." He pointed to the plastic tag containing a red plastic strip that read *CHIP 2.1.* "My wife Lizzie does the financials for the zoology department at Browning."

"I remember. She and I met at that the Fourth of July picnic last summer."

"Yeah. She says you're good folk. I agree, for what it's worth. Anyway, you wouldn't believe the crap they pull at that place. She had to keep an audit trail on those tags. They only used them on dogs for a big Army contract."

Sam had recognized the name of the CHIP project on the tag but hadn't said anything to Otis. He wanted to talk to Allen about it first. This tag connected the murders, or at least the body dump, to Allen's workplace and, just maybe, to the bite marks on Eric Bell's legs. That wasn't good. Maybe Otis knew something through his wife. "This was a squirrel habitat. Could they have used it for the dogs, too?"

"I don't think so. She's always complaining about the asshole in charge of the dogs, some jerk named Zarnoff or something."

"Sarnok."

"That's it. There's something about those dogs that ain't right. There was a rumor that one of them went berserk and attacked a graduate student. Put her in the hospital. Supposedly this Sarnok pulled strings and hushed it all up. Anyway, they was real careful with them dogs after that. They got their own, special habitat that's all secure. There's electrified fences and everything."

And Allen works there, with these dogs. And maybe a serial killer. Terrific. "Well, then, why is this tag in the squirrel lady's farm? Maybe I should ask Dr. Eckhorn."

That got him a snort from Otis. "For sure, you won't get nothing out of her. She's nuts."

"Then I should interview this Sarnok dude."

"Good luck with that. Lizzie told me that no matter what words came out of his mouth, what he's really saying is, 'You're stupid. I'm smart. Kiss my butt.' A real asshole."

Sam let a grim smile bend his lips. "He can't pull that crap on me. I can be an asshole, too, and I'm an asshole with a badge." He sighed and stretched again. "Shall we call it a night?"

"I'll stay as long as you do."

Sam glanced at his watch. "It's almost seven. Go home to your family. We can finish this up tomorrow morning. Not that I expect to find anything more." If I hurry, I could still have some time to talk to Allen.

"I spoke to the missus earlier. She said to invite you over for some home cooking tonight."

Sam hesitated. He didn't have any reason to think Otis would care he was gay, but long habit made him prevaricate. "That's really nice of her. Please tell her thank you for me, but I just want to get home, shower, and crash." He sniffed at his armpit and planted a rueful grin on his face. "I'm not fit for civilized company right now." That should be a semi-plausible excuse that didn't say, "My boyfriend is waiting for me."

"Lizzie won't care none. If it frets you, you can always use our shower."

"I really do appreciate the offer, Otis. Truly. But I can't tonight." Home cooking sounded good, but he needed Allen.

Otis's eyebrows went up. "If you got other plans, that's okay. We don't mean to force ourselves on you or nothing, but she'll want to know you're going to have a real meal tonight. No junk food."

"I will. I promise. Maybe we can get together another time, when we can be more relaxed. And when I smell better."

Otis nodded. "We'd like that. And there ain't never nothing wrong with sweat from good, honest work." He

83

hesitated, and then ventured, "If you got a friend, bring them along, too."

"No girlfriend, I'm afraid. Not much social life since I moved here, in fact." He couldn't look at Otis. He wished he was back in LA where he didn't have to lie.

Otis seemed about to say something more, but before he could speak Sam continued, "I really do appreciate your help. I know today was your day off. This is service above and beyond."

"I told you. I got your back. We all do." Otis locked eyes with him. "You ever need to talk, about this case or anything else, just say so. I mean it. You can trust me."

"Thanks, Otis. I appreciate you. Now get home to Lizzie. And don't forget to thank her for me."

"I will. And you take care of yourself, you hear? Get some sleep."

As the older man lumbered out, a cold blast of air ruffled through the garage. Sam pulled out his phone and sent a text to Allen. *I'll b home in 20. u there?* He shrugged into his leather jacket, and his phone buzzed. He answered, expecting Allen. "Hey, how are you?"

The ME's voice answered, "Overworked and under-appreciated, thank you very much."

Shit. Changing gears, Sam said, "Well, *I* appreciate you. What's up?"

"I thought you'd want to know. I asked the state ME to run the prints from that hand through the FBI. I just got back to the office and found a fax from their fingerprint database."

"IAFIS. I know it."

"Yes. Well, we have a positive ID on one of our victims, a Walter Sedgewick, nineteen, late of San Antonio, Texas."

"Interesting. Why were his prints on file?"

The speaker emitted sounds of paper shuffling. "His father is in the Air Force. It appears to have something to do with that. I took the liberty of checking with a colleague at Browning. Mr. Sedgewick was a student there."

"Good to know." *Why is he telling me this tonight instead of at our scheduled meeting tomorrow?* "Anything else?"

"Given what you told me about our other victim's sexual preferences, I made further inquiry. Mr. Sedgewick was also a documented homosexual."

Sam's mouth hardened. *It's an* orientation, *not a preference, asshole.* "I wasn't aware that gay people carried a special ID documenting their orientation, sir."

Twilling's voice turned prim. "I was referring to a *documented* charge of public indecency. The arresting officer was quite clear, I assure you."

He'd heard scuttlebutt that the Chief had created a vice unit that was targeting gays. Good thing Sam had been careful and not come out at work. "Well, that's useful information to have. Thanks for letting me know."

"You're welcome, Detective. I'll see you at eleven tomorrow. Don't be late." Twilling closed the connection without saying goodbye. The jerk. Sam wanted to tell him about the animal bones they'd found. That could wait until tomorrow, but he first wanted to be sure they were just squirrels.

His to-do list buzzed through his head. Report in to the Chief. Finish sifting the evidence here. Interview Sarnok. Maybe he'd see Allen then, too. Meet with Twilling. Go to the Pride Center to check on Sedgewick. That was a new one.

His phone chimed again, and this time it was a text from Allen. *Home working on big term paper. Can't come 2nite. Maybe 2morrow?*

Sam wilted with disappointment. Anticipation of spending the evening with Allen had kept him going all day.

Wait. If Allen's car wasn't working, he must have walked home. In the dark. Annoyance furrowed Sam's brow.

I warned him about the danger. He chewed the side of his mouth. *Don't push. He's an adult, capable of making his own decisions. Don't drive him away by being over-protective.*

He re-read Allen's text. Tomorrow would have to do. He used his thumb to type OK, and then stopped. Should he add "I love you?" His index finger hesitated over the send key, then he pressed it, adding nothing.

Damn it, he wasn't fourteen. It wasn't healthy to pretend he didn't have feelings. Next time they were alone together, he'd tell Allen.

Chapter 10

0830, Tuesday, October 30

Sam circled the parking lot, scoping out the Canine Research Facility. Sure enough, an eight-foot chain link fence topped with concertina wire extended from the rear of the building. A dense scrabble of bushes and other scrub hid whatever lay behind. Red danger signs warned the barrier was electrified and that trespassers would be prosecuted. Otis was right. It gave at least the outward appearance of elevated security.

The lab building was a gleaming structure of glass, burnished aluminum, and concrete that towered three stories over a manicured landscape. Sam rolled to a stop and killed his engine. He thought about texting Allen, but his car wasn't in the lot. He might still be at his apartment, working on his paper or asleep. Time for that later.

A receptionist sitting behind an ash-colored desk looked up when he entered the lobby. "How can I assist you, sir?"

Sam showed her his badge and then hung it around his neck. "I'm Detective Sam Sondergard of the Hollenbeck Police Department. I'd like to speak with Dr. Edwin Sarnok, please."

"Is Dr. Sarnok expecting you?"

"No."

Her mouth made a little o-shape. "May I tell his assistant what this is regarding?"

"The CHIP lab came up in an investigation. I need some background information. He's the director, right?"

She pushed on buttons her phone and whispered into her headset. "Dr. Sarnok's assistant, Mrs. Eberhard, will see you. If you'll have a seat, she'll be here in a moment to escort you to her office."

Just what he needed. Some petty bureaucrat wasting his time. Still, the receptionist couldn't do anything about it. "Thank you." Her phone chimed, but she nodded to him before answering.

Sam sauntered around the lobby and paused at the building directory. Interesting. There was only one entry for the entire third floor, "Army Intelligence Team." Allen wasn't even listed, but the CHIP kennel was in room 1C12. From the map, that must mean first floor, corridor C, room twelve.

Footsteps tap-tapped across the lobby, and Sam turned to face the newcomer.

A stout, middle-aged woman, her hair cropped in a short, efficient cut, greeted him with a smile and cold eyes that would have chilled Satan's heart. "Good morning, officer. I'm Mrs. Eberhard. Will you follow me, please?"

She turned and walked away without waiting for an answer or for him to introduce himself. Sam's face heated, and he took calming breaths as he let her lead him down a hall. They passed through double glass doors, a waiting room, and into a spacious office containing an immaculate desk and a single, stiff-backed guest chair. A discrete silver cross hanging on one wall was the only decoration.

She perched behind the desk and gave him another smile. Sam could swear the temperature dropped ten degrees. She folded her fingers as if in prayer and asked, "Now, what is your business here, officer?"

Sam reached into his pocket and placed a business card on her desk. "I'm Detective Sam Sondergard of the Hollenbeck Police Department, Mrs....Eberhard, is it?"

She picked up his card between thumb and forefinger as if afraid it might contain a deadly virus. "That's right, officer."

"I'm a detective, ma'am. May I sit?"

"If you wish, although I doubt you'll be here long." She pushed his card to one side of her desk and resumed her prayerful position. "Now, tell me your business."

Sam reached inside a jacket pocket and pulled out the evidence bag with the CHIP tag. "We found this at a crime scene, ma'am. Do you recognize it?"

"It looks like one of ours. That's impossible, of course."

"Why do you say that?"

"Because we have strict audit controls on those tags. May I see it?"

"I can't let you handle it because of chain of custody issues. But you may examine it while I hold it."

She sat a bit straighter. "I doubt that will be necessary. Does it have any numbers on it?"

"It says 2.1, right under 'Browning State College Department of Zoology.'"

"That's sufficient. The 'two' would refer to second generation animals, and the 'one' would be the birth order. That's if it were one of ours, but it's not. We disposed of all of those animals over three years ago, and our protocols called for the destruction of the tags at the same time. This one is a forgery."

"That doesn't make sense. Why would anyone forge a dog tag?"

"You're the detective, not me, officer. Will there be anything else?"

So she did hear me say I was a detective, despite calling me 'officer.' How does Allen put up with these people? "I'll need to verify the destruction by examining your records."

"I can't authorize that. The Army has classified our records secret." This time her smile was triumphant.

"I can get a search warrant. It might shut down this place for a couple of weeks while we look for evidence. You know, to be sure we got everything." *Take that, dragon lady.*

Her eyes narrowed. "Perhaps Dr. Sarnok might be able to arrange something. But you'd have to speak with him."

"I want to talk to him anyway, about other evidence we've found. On the bodies of the murder victims. If one of your experimental animals is loose in the community, it might be connected to my investigation."

"That's ridiculous. Our animals are strictly controlled, and they're harmless in any case." She sniffed. "Murders, indeed." But then she opened a drawer and pulled out an appointment book. "Dr. Sarnok could see you two weeks from this Friday. Will that do?"

"I can have a warrant by close of business today. Perhaps he and I can talk while we conduct our search."

She glared at him and let silence stretch for a few seconds. Finally, she said, "He's out of town today. I suppose I could move things around and pencil you in for ten-thirty, tomorrow. Will that do?"

It sounded like it would have to. "Yes."

She jotted a notation. "Don't be late."

"I won't." *Sarnok better not be, either.* "Don't show me out. I can find my own way."

She'd already picked up her phone and wasn't paying attention.

Sam wanted to slam the door, but the pneumatic hinge foiled him. Eberhard's office was 1A01. From the map at the front, a connecting corridor ran to the B and C corridors. It wouldn't hurt to scout the interior of this place.

The C corridor was more utilitarian than the others. The floors were concrete, and painted steel doors lined the hall instead of glass walls. The smell was different, too. There were definitely animals nearby.

One of the doors opened, and an African-American woman in scrubs emerged, followed by a golden retriever and Allen. Sam's heart quickened, and a grin split his features. "Hey, fancy seeing you here."

Surprise and then glee skated across Allen's features. "Sam! What are *you* doing here?" He turned to his female companion. "Trish, this is Sam. I've told you about him."

She put her hands on her hips and examined Sam head-to-toe before turning back to Allen with a stern expression. "Child, you been talking about nothing *but* this man for the last two weeks, and you didn't think to mention he was a *brother*?"

Allen slapped a palm to his check, bugged his eyes out, and dropped his jaw in an exaggerated look of horror. "Oh, no! You mean...It *can't* be. Sam, you're a *negro?*" He rolled his eyes, faced Trish, and ticked off points with his fingers. "I told you that he cares for me, that he's smart, and that he has a wicked sense of humor. That's the important stuff."

"You forgot sexy, child. You must have mentioned that a million times." She beamed at Sam. "Don't you give him no never mind. This one's smart as a whip, but he can be a little slow when it comes to people. Like introducing folks. My name's Trish."

"Sam." He offered his hand.

She brushed aside his extended arm and enveloped him a bear hug. "So good to finally *meet* you, honey. Allen has told me all *about* you. He won't shut up, in fact. I feel like you're an old friend."

He patted her ample back. She was just like the women in his Momma's church back in LA. If he could put up with them, Trish would be no problem at all.

Allen's features turned crimson. "Stop it, Trish." He stepped up to Sam and pecked him on the cheek.

The dog that was with him had sat on its haunches and watched the whole exchange up until now, but when they kissed, it circled Sam, sniffing at his shoes and pants.

Sam squatted down and let it smell his hand. When it started giving him slobbery kisses on his face, he laughed and ruffled its ears. "This must be Teena?"

"Isn't she beautiful? Good thing she approves of you. I guess I get to keep you."

Teena barked and licked Sam's hand, her tail whirling like an insane, furry metronome. She nuzzled him some more, and then gave Allen a little push, as if to move them closer together.

Trish clasped her hands. "Ain't that the cutest thing ever? Look at her match-making."

Allen snapped Teena's leash. "Sit!" Her tail drooped between her legs and her head sagged, but she obeyed. "That's a *good* dog." Allen gave her a treat from his pocket, and her ears perked up. He turned to Sam and asked, "So what brings you here, anyway? I thought you'd be working on your case."

"That's why I'm here." He showed them the evidence bag. "We found this at our crime scene."

Trish's smile disappeared. "You working those awful murders? We said a prayer at church for the poor victims. For the police, too." She peered at the tag. "That's one of them *demon* dogs' tags. The second generation."

Sam quirked an eyebrow. "Talk to me."

"Back then, the dogs weren't nothing like the ones here now. One of the third generation almost killed a graduate student. Put the poor thing in the hospital for weeks."

"What happened to those animals? Mrs. Eberhard implied they were euthanized."

"Eberhard. That woman. More like ever-hard, you ask me." She sniffed. "Weren't the dogs fault what Dr. Sarnok did to them, but they had to be put down. They were vicious."

If one of the dogs got in the hands of his killer, that might explain the bites on Eric Bell's legs. Given the security around the animals, the paper trail on their destruction might lead him to his killer. "Did they keep records on how they disposed of them? Did they do it here?"

"Don't know. It was all hushed up. The staff vet Dr. Harzig could tell you." A frown furrowed her brow. "I wouldn't want to tell tales out of church, but if I were you, I wouldn't trust the people what run this place any further than you can spit." She hesitated. "Mrs. Bateman, though, she's different. She told me once she knows things that would curl the hair on a jackrabbit's nose."

That would be Otis's wife. He'd mentioned she thought something was amiss. "What kinds of things?"

"She handles the money. Can't hide much from them that controls the purse strings."

True that. But he'd need probable cause before he could look at financial or other records. Random gossip wouldn't pass muster, and if he didn't follow protocol, the DA might not be able to use whatever evidence he developed. Another problem for later. This investigation was growing tentacles on tentacles.

Allen spoke up. "I really should get to work. Dr. Sarnok has given me a shit load of tests today, and I've got my term paper to finish. If I don't get my ass in gear, I'll be in the office all night working."

Sam was still determined to have that talk with Allen, but not in front of Trish. "So you won't be over for dinner tonight?"

Allen's expression turned hangdog. "I really don't see how. What books aren't in my office are at my place. I've got at least eight hours of work to do tonight, so I wouldn't be getting there before one or two in the morning at the soonest."

"Your car still broke?"

Allen's face flushed, and his eyes threatened to roll out of his head. "Not that again," he snapped. "I told you. I'm safe."

"Damn it, there's a serial killer out there." He clenched his jaws. *Temper. Control your temper.*

"Look. I've been taking care of myself since I was ten. I know you're a cop and all, but it's not your job to be my fairy godfather."

"You're right. I'm a cop, so I'm the expert. If we were, I don't know, buying dog biscuits, you'd be the expert." Sam knew at once it was the wrong thing to say, but didn't know how to take it back.

"*Dog biscuits*? Is that what you think of me?"

"I'm sorry." *How to explain?* "It's just I don't want to lose you like I lost Misha."

That made Trisha cluck her tongue, and Sam realized he'd just dug himself a deeper hole.

Allen snapped, "I'm not Misha. I'm *me*. Allen." He snatched at Teena's leash and headed toward the door, but she whimpered and stayed anchored to the floor. Her doleful gaze swiveled between Allen and Sam. "Teena, what's wrong with you? We've got work to do."

Trisha put her hands on her hips. "She's one smart puppy. Plain as day, she's telling you two to kiss and make up."

Allen's mouth formed a hard line, and he glared at Trisha, then at Sam. But his features softened, and he heaved a sigh. "Okay, she's right. You, too, Trish. Look, I'm sorry I snapped at you, but you've got to give me some respect. Don't tell me what to do."

Sam wanted to say he was still right, but instead squeezed out an apology. "I'm sorry." That was safer.

"Okay, then. Let me finish my term paper tonight, and you do whatever you need to for your investigation. I'll cook dinner at your place tomorrow night, and we'll talk then. Does that work?"

It sounded like it would have to. "Sure. You've got your key." How the hell was he going to get across town tomorrow with his car not working? *Don't ask.*

Allen felt in his pocket and nodded. "Key's right here." He pecked Sam on the cheek, turned on his heel and left, dragging Teena behind him.

Sam stared at his retreating back, his mouth twisted into an angry grimace. He'd pushed too hard, sure, but damn it, Allen shouldn't have gone off on him, either. Maybe cooling things for a day or so would be healthy.

Or maybe this would turn out to be just a fling, after all.

Chapter 11

1530, Tuesday, October 30

Chief "Bump" Hartman pushed into Teaser's Cabaret and paused for his eyes to adjust to the dim, red lighting. The bar stank of cigarettes, old sweat, and stale beer. Cheesy disco music thumped from overhead speakers. A bored dancer, clad only in a g-string, clung to a pole in the middle of the bar shaking her moneymaker and chewing gum.

A middle-aged woman with hair the size of Texas and wearing a black dress that crawled up her ass slinked up to him. "Good to see you, Bump." Her voice reminded him of warm maple syrup, except syrup couldn't be sarcastic.

"Hi, Lorna. Looks kind of slow today."

She patted the straw-colored curls that poofed around her head and surveyed the bar. Half a dozen overweight men sat at solitary tables. Their pig-like eyes were riveted on the dancer, who blew a huge pink bubble and then resumed her half-assed dance. "Just the usual losers. These guys can barely afford the cover, let alone tip the girls. The shift just changed at the plant. Give it twenty minutes. It'll pick up."

Hartman shrugged. He could care less about Lorna's business, or her girls for that matter. He never understood why the mayor liked this place. Naked women flopping around just repulsed him. "Is Henry here?"

"Yeah, the mayor's back in his private room, where he can see but not be seen." She pooched out her lips and made kissing sounds. "Go do your thing, sugar. Don't get your nose too far up his ass."

"God damn it, Lorna. You can show me some respect, or I'll have vice in here and close you down."

"Like our good friend the mayor would permit *that*. Fuck you, Mr. Chief Of Ass-kissing Police, and the horse you rode in on."

Hartman glared at her, but she'd already turned to greet two men entering the bar. They must be construction workers, from their worn jeans to the muscles bulging out of their plaid shirts. It wouldn't do for the good citizens of Hollenbeck to see him in a stripper bar. He sneaked a secret glance at the tight ass on one of the workers, clenched his jaw, and stomped to the back room.

Hartman pushed into the mayor's private room at the back of the bar. The heavy scent of cheap cologne and dirty socks hung in the air. The mayor rested in a Barcalounger, his feet up and his shoes off, scratching his belly. He was short, with tousled hair and a winning smile that said, "I'm your best buddy."

He wasn't smiling at the moment. A half-empty fifth of Scotch and a bucket of ice sat on a table next to him. He slurped at his drink and didn't take his eyes off the dancer on the other side of the one-way mirror. "About time you got here, Bump."

"I came as soon as you called, sir."

"Yeah, whatever." He waved at the battered folding chairs next to him. "Have seat and pour yourself a drink. Pour me one, while you're at it."

Hartman sat and accepted the mayor's glass. "I can't drink. I'm on duty." He scooped up fresh ice and poured three fingers into the glass.

"Don't be such a tight ass. Look at that sweet piece of tail out there. Wouldn't you like to pork her?"

That was the last thing Hartman wanted. "Did you want a report on the investigation or not?"

The mayor's mouth soured. He tipped his head back and closed his eyes. "Sure. Talk to me."

"I've pretty much got it contained, with that *African* Sondergard running it. Lazy ass wanted to pass it off to the state police, but I chewed him good. For a while, it looked like the College was going to throw a monkey wrench into things, but I fixed that, too."

The mayor's eyebrows went up. "Monkey wrench how?"

"Well, the place we found all them bodies is owned by the College. That makes it state property, so if they got pissy about it they could call in the state police."

"No state involvement, god damn it. I told you — "

Hartman held up a hand, palm forward. "I *told* you I took care of it. The old fart what runs the campus cops agreed to just assign a liaison to Sondergard. No state police. I made a contribution to his retirement fund, if you catch my drift."

"Subtle." The mayor poured himself another drink. "We can't afford publicity right now."

"I don't see that, Henry." Hartman savored the taste of the mayor's first name in his mouth, as though the intimacy gave him power. "If we solve this case, won't that make us look good? Doesn't that fall right into our plans?"

"*My* plans, Bump. These are my plans, and don't you forget it." He sucked at his drink. "Look, suppose it turns out that someone local is the killer. That means you ain't been doing your job and, by extension, I ain't been doing mine. If, on the other hand, the killer is from one of them librul big cities, that fits with my next move. Then it's them librul's fault, not righteous plain folk like us. So we got to make sure the investigation works out that way."

"I get that. But so what if we solve the case? What's so awful about some good publicity? How can that hurt when you run for Congress next year?" It was always about him and his career. Self-centered asshole. Solving this case would be good for *Hartman.* Why should he give a dry fuck what was good for the mayor?

"Good publicity or bad draws attention to us. We can't afford that right now. I don't want nobody snooping around here. If you had two brain cells to click together, you'd see it. It's bad enough that you bought that Mercedes S-type. People is going to wonder where you got that kind of money."

Who did he think he was, calling him stupid and telling him how to spend his money? The prick. "It's nobody's business. Besides, I saved it up."

"Like shit. Not on what the city pays you. All it takes is some bleeding-heart librul reporter digging around to blow our whole deal here. Better we close this case with no publicity, or leave it open and blame them bodies on out-of-towners. Don't screw up." He re-filled his glass. "Once I'm in Congress, you can do whatever dumbass thing you want."

Hartman's throat tightened. He couldn't fucking wait for the mayor to be in Congress and out of his hair. Before he could argue, though, the door opened and that smug SOB Sarnok pranced into the room.

"Good afternoon, Mayor. Chief." He barely nodded at Hartman. "What's so important that we needed to meet? I just returned from consulting with the Army brass in Arizona, and I get this text ordering me here. I'm not at your beck and call, you know. I'm an important research scientist."

The mayor snorted. "You got that Army contract because of my connections, and don't you forget it. I need more cash for my media team. They're producing a documentary on me for the Fox outlet in the capital. Make it happen."

"Really, these payments from the grant are getting harder to explain. The department's financial manager has been asking questions. I think she's suspicious."

"She's just a clerk, right? A nobody. Fire her ass. Once I'm in Congress, you'll get ten times the grant money you got now. Don't worry, I'll remember the folks what help me." He glanced at Harman, and muttered, "I won't forget the ones that didn't follow through, neither."

Hartman scowled at the mayor's threat. Screw him. If the mayor could demand payment, so could he. "I've got some unexpected expenses, too. The ME's threatening to call in the state medical examiner on these murders. A few thousand would shut him up."

Sarnok turned to him and snapped, "I'll tell you who needs shut up. There's this police officer who showed up in my lab today and *bullied* my staff into getting an appointment with me tomorrow. I don't have time for this."

"Who was it?" *Didn't that fuckwad Sondergard say he was going to the lab?*

"Some angry black goon. He *threatened* my staff assistant. It's people like him who give the police a bad name."

"That's Sam Sondergard. He's the only African on the force. If he's getting uppity, I'll fire his ass."

The mayor waved a finger at him. "Bump, Bump. You never think things through."

"What you talking about? I been looking for a reason to get rid of him ever since I got this job. That bleeding heart who was chief before me hired him, so I've been stuck with him. But now we've got a civilian complaint."

The mayor rubbed his forehead and rolled his eyes. "He's the one in charge of the murder investigation, right?"

Who did that asshole mayor think he was, talking down to Hartman like he was a moron or something? He was the fucking chief of police. "That's right." He kept his voice even. He'd be the adult in the room.

"So, what's your plan if there's another murder, or if more bodies pile up? We've got, what, six already?"

"Why, I'll blame the officer in charge and fire — oh. You think I should keep him around as a scapegoat in case more victims pop up."

The mayor nodded. "I knew you'd figure it out if I led you by the nose. I mean, he's *African,* for fuck's sake. Probably Muslim, too. He's not from around here. Nobody's going to give a rat's ass if we fire him, especially if he screws up the investigation."

Hartman nodded. He liked it. The mayor was a devious asshole, but sometimes that was what you needed. "You mean *when* I fire him. He was in LA before he came here. Probably got gang connections, too. Okay, I'll keep him around for now. But I'm going to fire that boy, one way or another. I can't stand it when them people get uppity."

Chapter 12

1630, Tuesday, October 30

Allen slumped at his desk on the third floor of the zoology building and stared at the pile of test results from this morning. That asshole Sarnok insisted Allen code and enter them in the system today. When was he going to have time to finish his paper? The overhead fluorescent lights flickered and buzzed. He fingered the selfie of Sam and himself that he'd printed out last Friday and taped to his monitor. The big jerk. What Allen really wanted to do was make up.

In the next cubical, a sullen freshman announced to his teaching assistant that he was a business major and therefore didn't need to know the difference between glycogen and cellulose. Allen closed his eyes and rubbed his forehead. Maybe he should be grateful that he didn't have to teach the unwilling. All he had to do was satisfy the insatiable. The results weren't going to code themselves. He picked up the top sheet and hunched over his keyboard.

Two hours later, he turned over the last paper in the stack. The other GAs were long gone. The ancient radiators clanked, and rain drizzled against the windows. Allen stretched and checked his phone. No texts from Sam. He fingered the screen. Maybe a time out for a day was a good thing. They'd have dinner tomorrow, and everything would be fine.

A voice from just outside his cubicle made him jump. "What are you still doing here?" Seth Harzig, the department's staff veterinarian, slouched against the cubical entrance. He reeked of cigarettes, and his belly hung over his blue jeans. A fringe of beard and hair sprouted around his head like steel wool, as if he channeled Jerry Garcia.

"I had to code today's test results." Allen nodded at the stack of papers. "Just finished, in fact."

"You let that Sarnok push you around too much. I remember back before he got his big Army contract. He was still an asshole, but nobody had to kiss his butt."

Allen shrugged. "Well, he got the grant, and now it pays my stipend. It even built the research facility on south campus. So I can't really complain."

Harzig sidled closer and put a hand on Allen's shoulder. "You're too nice. What you need is to ease up. Drugs, sex, and rock and roll. When I was your age back in New York that was all I cared about."

And look where you are now. Allen chewed his lower lip. *Be kind.* "I'm not much into that kind of thing. Really, I love my research."

Harzig leaned forward, still squeezing Allen's shoulder. "Who's the guy in the picture?" A leer twisted his mouth. "Don't tell me you've got a boyfriend?"

Allen shrugged off his hand and stood. *Maybe if I say yes, he'll stop hitting on me. Not any of his business who Sam is, though.* "He's just someone I met a couple of weeks ago. A cop. We've gone out a few times."

Seth's eyebrows shot up. "A cop? That's butch. So you and he got big plans tonight?"

"No. He's working a case — those bodies from Dr. Eckhorn's habit."

"God, I read about that. She's been all weepy this week. Like anyone cares about ground squirrels." His face lit up. "If you don't have plans, you want to have dinner? Or some beers? Like I said, you need to lighten up."

Great. Still hitting on me. "Can't. I've got a big term paper that's due tomorrow. I'm headed home."

"Okay. Some other time. It's raining. You need a lift or anything?"

Allen didn't really want to walk in the rain. It would make Sam happy if he accepted. But, damn it, he had to learn he couldn't just give Allen orders. Plus Seth was creeping him out. "No, thanks. I'll be fine."

"Well, it's no big deal either way. Don't forget we've got the monthly health checks on the dogs tomorrow."

Right. Eight sharp. "I'll be there."

"See you then." Harzig hitched his pants up and waddled away.

Allen searched through the papers and empty Cheetos sacks on his desk, looking for his umbrella. Shit. He probably had two in his car and none in the office. And his junk heap of a car sat in the parking lot outside his apartment. He stuffed notes for his assignment into his briefcase, added the three references he'd need that weren't already in his apartment, and surveyed the office one last time. Satisfied he had everything, he slipped into a plastic rain slicker and pulled the hood over his head.

Outside, the rain had turned to a desultory drizzle. A low overcast reflected the street lamps, creating a claustrophobic ceiling over the campus. At least the temperatures were a little warmer. He pulled his raincoat tighter and struck out on his usual shortcut, across the intramural fields, the railroad tracks, and then through the old Eagles Cemetery. After that, it was only a few blocks to his apartment, leftovers, and a sleepless night working on his term paper.

A group of jocks had turned the lights on at the intramural field and were playing touch football in the mud. Allen recognized two guys who'd driven by the Tool Box last month, shouting catcalls at the patrons. That was all he needed tonight. He detoured around them to the far end.

He was just about to escape into the shadows of the railroad tracks when their football tumbled across the grass and came to rest not twenty feet from him.

One of the guys shouted. "Hey, dude. Toss us our ball, will you?"

This couldn't end well. Allen tried to ignore them.

"You! Doofus. Dig the dirt out of your ears."

Allen turned. He swallowed an angry retort. *Stay calm.*

One of the guys stood with hands on his hips, glaring at him. Mud smeared the guy's handsome face. He'd scraped his knee, and trickle of dried blood ran down his shin. "You too good to help us, or what? Throw our ball back this way."

Allen eyed the ball. Maybe if he tossed it to them, they'd leave him alone. He put his briefcase down and picked it up. It was hard and bulky in his hand. He reared back and flung it. It wobbled like a wounded duck and landed less than half the distance between Allen and the muddy-faced guy.

"Jesus. You throw like a fucking girl. What are you, a faggot?"

He started to run toward Allen, but another of the men held him back. "We got our ball. Come on. Let's play."

Allen picked up his briefcase and stomped through the squishy grass. *Fucking jerks.*

The cemetery was better. There were no people in it. At least, no living people. The dead were easier to get along with. They couldn't hurt you.

Allen strode between the tombstones and toward the statue that stood on a little hillock at the center of the graveyard. It looked like a monk, but an art history major he'd met at the Pride Center had told him it was a *pleurant*. She'd explained that in the Middle Ages nobility had hired professional mourners to attend funerals. These weepers —

pleurants — wore robes that covered their faces so no one could see their tears. Later, the wealthy had commissioned statues like the one here to adorn tombs.

Allen picked up his pace. Not much light leaked into the cemetery, and the temperature was dropping. He halted when he reached the statue. Condoms, crushed beer cans, and needles scattered at its base, and someone had defaced the weeping figure with obscene graffiti, painting an erect penis on the mourner's robes.

Allen heaved a shuddering sigh. Life just sucked sometimes. First his fight with Sam, then Harzig's creepy advances, the homophobic footballer, and now this. He just wanted to go to bed, pull the covers over his head, and make the world go away.

His briefcase dragged at his arm. Tomorrow would be better. He trudged on to the broken-down chain link fence at the edge of the cemetery and onto Jenkins Avenue. Six more blocks. He'd call Sam when he got to his apartment. Life couldn't really suck. Not with someone like Sam in it.

A battered blue van rattled by, spouting foul blue exhaust. It stopped a half block away, in front of a boarded-up warehouse. The door opened, and gray-haired, stooped man got out and limped to the back. He had a cast on one arm. A dog jumped out after him and scuttled behind him.

Allen stopped and gaped. For an instant, he thought Teena had escaped and was right here in front of him. But that couldn't be. Still...He squinted through the rain. The dog could have been her twin. Big head and yellow fur ticked with gray highlights. It — no *he* — saw him and scampered his way.

Allen squatted and let the animal sniff his hand. He ruffled its ears and murmured, "*Good* dog. Yeah, you're a good fellow, aren't you?" Damn. He *was* one of the CHIP dogs. The number 2.1 was tattooed to his right ear, and the left ear flopped in two pieces. Someone must have ripped the tag off, tearing the ear. "Poor thing. What happened to you?"

He glanced up at the man, who stood rubbing his cast and staring at them. The dog seemed tame enough, but so had all the early generation specimens. He'd read the reports. They'd act more or less normal, but then something would set them off, and they'd turn into vicious killers. This guy was lucky he'd not been attacked. Allen stood. He had to warn him, before it was too late.

The man's voice sounded like fingernails across rusty metal. "Spot! Don't bother the young fellow. You come here, dog."

Spot yipped, his tail drooped between his legs, and he skittered back to the van. The old fellow opened the rear door and pulled out a sack of groceries.

Allen approached. When he was a few feet short of the van, Spot ran back to him and planted more slobbery doggie kisses on his hand.

"Spot, stop that." the man wheezed. He shot an apologetic look at Allen. "Don't know what got into that animal." His face split in a gap-toothed smile. "Name's Bobby, by the way." He nodded to the dog. "The way he's making up to you, I reckon you're something special. He don't usually ken to most folk."

Allen stiffened his upper lip and clenched his nostrils. He was used to bad smells, but the odor coming from the van was something special. Or maybe it was Bobby. His teeth were edged in green, and his clothes looked like he'd spent the last month sleeping in mud. Never mind. That just made him more pathetic. The last thing he needed was an out-of-control, genetically engineered dog tearing him to shreds. "I'm Allen, Nice to meet you. Can I ask where you got this dog, sir?"

"You mean my Spot? I got him at the pound, that's where. He's my only friend." He flicked a finger at the dog who jumped in the back of the van.

His only friend. Allen could identify with that. "Sir, I think you might be in danger. I recognized the tattoo on his ear. It's what we use on our specially bred experimental animals."

"I got him at the pound, I tell you." Bobby's eyes narrowed. "You ain't trying to steal my Spot, is you?"

"No, sir. I'd never do that. But some of these dogs, the ones with numbers starting with one through six, they turned out to be dangerous. Your dog's tattoo starts with a two. It's unsafe to let him run free." Sarnok euthanized them, the bastard. They were his mistake, but the dogs paid. Maybe Allen could save this one *and* the old man.

"Spot ain't never hurt no one. I got him at the pound, I tell you." Bobby pointed to the van. "I got papers on him. They're right there, in the back. They'll prove he's just a stray mutt what the dog catcher picked up." He took a step toward the van, slipped, and fell to the pavement, banging his cast against the bumper. "Jesus," he shrieked. "Now look what you made me do."

Allen winced and offered a hand. "Let me help you up."

Bobby took his offer of help and let Allen lift him to his feet. "God, that hurts," he whimpered. "I tell you the papers is in there, right underneath them pizza boxes. Check them out."

Allen looked at the van. The smell roiled his stomach and he swallowed the saliva that flooded his mouth. Now would not be the time to hurl.

Spot sat inside on his haunches, his tail thumping on the floorboards and his tongue lolly-gagging from his mouth. He looked just like Teena. The papers couldn't prove anything, but maybe it would save time arguing to at least look at them. Allen held his breath and climbed into the stench.

A shadow fell across the back. He turned just in time to see Bobby swing the tire iron at his head and to think Sam had been right. An instant of searing pain ended in blackness.

Chapter 13

0900, Wednesday, October 31

Sam pulled into the strip mall's parking lot and shaded his eyes against the glare of the morning sun. He stopped and scanned the store fronts, looking for the Hollenbeck Pride Center. That had to be it, wedged between a tattoo parlor and an Asian food take-out joint. The rainbow flags and *Silence=Death* posters were hard to miss.

When he eased his car forward, it bounced into a chuck-hole filled with rain water from last night's storm. Sam winced as his suspension squeaked and the car scraped against the pavement. He pulled into a parking space and took in the dismal surroundings. Flyers, discarded take-out sacks, and who-knew-what-else slumped in soggy heaps against the curb. A crack ran diagonally across the window to the Pride Center, repaired with duct tape. Two doors down, a dumpster overflowed with trash.

He stepped out into the crisp fall morning and pinched his nose against the stench of stale grease, garlic, and uncollected garbage. He couldn't help but contrast this dump against the gleaming LGBT center in Los Angeles. Still, it could be worse. At least Hollenbeck *had* a place for the gay kids who were trapped here and for volunteers like Allen.

Thinking of Allen, he paused to check his cell phone. Still no texts. His mouth formed a hard line. Allen *knew* Sam was worried about him. You'd think he'd at least have the courtesy to text him and let him know he got home safely last night. Well, Sam could be stubborn, too. Tonight. They'd have it out face-to-face tonight. He put his phone back in his pocket and pushed into the Center.

Inside, a young man wearing mascara sat behind a table, leafing through a magazine. His hair was the same spiked style as Allen's, except that Allen's wasn't yellow with orange tips. Thank god for small miracles. The guy's head bounced as he lip-synched to a tinny version of *Take a Chance on Me* escaping from the earbuds of his iPod. A half dozen rings pierced his right ear, a wire ran through his left eyebrow, and silver bead protruded from the dimple in his chin.

Sam put his hands on the counter and cleared his throat.

The kid just turned the page of his porno magazine and didn't look up.

"I could use some help." Sam rapped on the counter with his knuckles.

Still no response.

Time for his crowd control voice. "Excuse me."

The guy jumped, and his spikey hair bounced. "You don't have to shout, man," he answered in a Texas twang. He slipped off his ear buds, and his gaze raked over Sam's body. "Well, shut my mouth. Ain't you just the most butch thing I've seen in a week of Sundays? What can old Charlie do for *you?*"

Sam showed him his badge. "I'm Detective Sam Sondergard with the Hollenbeck Police Department. I'd like to ask you a few questions."

"You're a cop, too? Fiddle dee dee, right here in the Pride Center. Darling, you can ask me anything." He bent a corner of his magazine and slipped it in a drawer.

Sam flipped open his notebook. "Can you tell me a little bit about what you do here, Charlie?"

Charlie grinned and leaned forward, resting his elbows on the counter and his chin in his upturned palms. One bejeweled toe extended from under the table and traced circles on the floor while he fluttered his eyelids. "Well, Officer, you know this is a *gay pride* center, right?"

"That's what the sign says."

"I knew you were a smart one, hon," he leered. "You ever go to the bars? I just know I've seen you someplace."

"This isn't about where I go." Sam frowned. "Isn't the gay helpline staffed here?"

"You lookin' for help, sugar? You just ask ol' Charlie and she'll give you mo' help than you ever imagined." His hips rotated, and he gave Sam a lascivious grin.

Sam scowled and slapped a photograph of one of the decaying torsos from the body dump on the counter. "I'm trying to find who did this."

Charlie shrieked and reeled back. "You get that nasty picture away from me, you hear?" He held his hands over his face and trembled. "I don't need to see no sick shit like that! Who you think you are, anyway?"

Sam replaced the photo in his notebook. "So, are you ready to answer some questions?"

A slim, balding man in khakis and a crisp, button-down shirt emerged from the back. "What's going on out here?" He put an arm around Charlie. "Shush, now. It's all right. He can't hurt you." He glared at Sam. "Who are you? Are you harassing him?"

Why did it always have to be so complicated? "Detective Sam Sondergard, Hollenbeck PD." He displayed his badge again. "I'm investigating some suspicious deaths that have recently come to light — "

"You mean those bodies over in Oak Crest? What's that got do with us?"

"I'm not sure, sir. So far, we've only been able to identify one of the remains. It turns out he was gay, a student at Browning." Sam paused to pull out another list. "In cases like this, the first thing we do is look at open missing person cases.

I hoped you might review this list and tell me if you recognize any of the names."

The bald man's jaw muscles jumped. He scanned Sam from head to toe with narrowed eyes, his expression looking as if he'd bitten into an apple and found Sam inside. "I can't violate the confidentiality of our clients."

"Understood. I'm not asking for that. I'm just trying to rule out potential victims." Or rule them in. "Would you at least look at the list?" He held it out.

Baldy scowled . "Let me see your badge again, please." He inspected it, and then handed it back. "Very well." He held out his hand. "The name's Marc Haddock. I'm executive director here."

"Pleased to meet you." The guy's grip with solid, without trying for a macho, knuckle-crushing contest.

"Let's do this in my office. If you'll follow me, Officer."

Sam cringed at the "Officer," but decided to let it pass. He followed the man through a hallway cluttered with boxes to a cramped, windowless room in the back.

Mark pointed to a folding chair sitting next to a desk where file folders teetered in precarious piles. He plopped into a tattered executive chair and glared at Sam. "I won't tolerate any police harassment. Let me make that clear, right off."

"I just need your help, sir. I don't want to harass anybody. I promise you."

"All right, then. What did you do that set Charlie off?"

"I showed him this." He handed over the photo.

Marc examined it and pushed it back across his desk. "Gruesome. Was it really necessary to show that to Charlie?"

"I was having some trouble getting his attention."

Marc gave a little snort. "Okay, I get that. Charley's about two sandwiches short of a picnic. For sure, you've got my attention." He peered at Sam's face. "You know, you look real familiar. Do you maybe know a guy named Allen?"

Sam nodded, a smile tickling his features before he remembered to be mad and squelched it.

"Yeah, you're Allen's new squeeze, right? Sam. He said he was dating a cop and he showed me a selfie of the two of you."

"Allen and I have been seeing each other, yes." *Damn it, this wasn't about him. Steady. You get more flies with sugar than with a Sig-Sauer.*

Mark nodded. "Allen's great. We all love him here." He turned a furious scowl on Sam. "You be good to him, you hear? He deserves it!"

What Allen and I do is none of your frigging business. Besides, I was trying to take care of him, and he blew me off. Sam controlled his breathing. *Stay on topic.* "Allen's terrific. I couldn't agree more. Now, I wonder if you could take a look at my list?"

"Sure, sure." He put on reading glasses and peered at the paper Sam handed him. "Say, you don't know where Allen's at, do you? Our regular volunteer couldn't make it last night, and we tried to get him to come in. He didn't answer his phone." He winked. "Or were you keeping him busy?"

Sam frowned. "We were both working last night. Allen had a term paper due today. I think he planned on working on that." Worry churned inside despite his calm tone. Damn it, if Allen cared, he would have called. Sam touched his cell phone. Screw it. *He'd* call Allen as soon as he was done here. A relationship wasn't a pissing contest to see who'd give in first. Besides, he needed a good talking to.

"It's not like him to not answer his phone." Mark shrugged. "I recognize quite a few names on this list. Some of them spent time in our group home. Eric Bell, for instance.

114

But he told us he was going home. He's from one of the little towns around here. I'd have to check his file."

Sam's gut chilled at the mention of Eric. He wasn't going to let Allen wind up rotting in an Alley. "I regret to inform you that Mr. Bell is deceased."

Marc blanched. "My god. Eric? He's the one you identified? Are you sure?"

"The ME got a positive ID off his dental records. I'm sorry." Sam's throat tightened, and his fingers trembled. What was wrong with him? Usually he was able to keep a professional detachment when discussing victims.

"Jesus. These kids show up here, and then they disappear. A lot of them live on the streets, or hitch rides to bigger cities. Like *that* will make their lives better." He chewed on his lip. "I recognize several names. Walt Sedgewick is another. He's a student at Browning. He got swept up in a vice sweep about a month ago. His ass wipe Air Force colonel father cut off his funding and got him kicked out of his fraternity. Last I heard, he was living on the streets." He shook his head. "We get all types, you know? From drama queens like Charlie to beefy, weight-lifter types. But the ones I recognize here are like Eric and Walt: boy-next-door types. Fit, but slim. Clones."

Like Allen. Fuck. What's he thinking walking around town alone at night? "I know the type."

Marc nodded. "Let me pull our files and see what I can find. I'll make it my top priority."

"Thank you, sir. I appreciate it."

"Yeah. Jesus, poor Eric. Was that him in the photo?"

"No. That victim is still unidentified." *Along with a shitload of others. Hope some of the kids on that list are still breathing.*

"Yeah. You got a card? I should have something for you by this afternoon."

Sam wrote his personal cell phone on the back of his HPD business card and handed it to Marc. "If you think of anything else, give me a call. Anytime."

"I'll do that." He stood. "Do you need anything else?"

Sam paused, and then answered, "How about your halfway house? The kids there might remember something, or know something."

"It's been empty the last month or so. When the weather's good, they tend to stay on the streets. You know. Because hustling."

Fat chance any of the street kids would talk to a cop, not after Vice had been harassing them. "Well, if you could put the word out we're looking for information, I'd be grateful."

"Will do. They're pretty skittish, though, even with me."

"Thanks. I'll be in touch." Sam shook his hand and wound his way back to the front of the storefront.

Charlie wolf-whistled at him as he left. "Y'all come back any time, stud! Just don't show old Charlie no more of them nasty pics."

Sam grimaced and waved at him. Back in his car he pulled out his phone and called Allen's cell. Still no answer, damn him. He left a message to call him back and then opened the directory entry for Allen's roommate, Stan. The guy was a jerk, but Sam pressed call anyway.

"Hello?" Stan's normal tone appeared to be sullen.

"Hey. This is Sam. Is Allen there?"

"Nah. He didn't come home last night." A pause. "I figured he was with you."

"No." *What the fuck was going on?* "You're sure didn't come home at all last night?"

"He wasn't here when I went to bed at eleven. He wasn't here when I got up at eight. The kitchen table's still all covered with crap from that paper he was working on. You figure it out."

The guy had the personality of a potato. An obnoxious potato. "He didn't get a call from his family or anything, did he?"

"Not that I know. You want I should take a message?"

"No. Wait, yes. Have him call me, okay?"

"Will do. I'll post a note on his door."

"Thanks. Bye." Stan had already hung up. Sam stared at his phone. *Where the fuck is Allen? His car's on the fritz. He's not answering his phone.* Sam thought about calling the emergency room, but then felt foolish. Maybe he just fell asleep in his office, working on his paper. Didn't he say he might do that?

Sam glanced at his watch. Shit! Almost time for his appointment back at the Canine Research Facility. He started the engine and sped out of the parking lot onto Jenkins.

Now that he thought about it, he was sure Allen was there right now. With any luck, he could check in with him before his meeting with Sarnok. Sam stomped on the accelerator and water from a chuckhole sprayed across the windshield, momentarily blinding him.

He braked for a beat-up blue van that crept down the street, leaving a trail of foul blue exhaust. He honked, but the asshole wouldn't pull over. At the first break in the traffic, he swerved into the other lane and sped around. So much for seeing Allen before the meeting. Damn him, anyway. Why didn't he *call*?

Chapter 14

1043, Wednesday, October 31

Sam fidgeted in his chair and glared at the gleaming conference room. Where the hell was Sarnok? If he'd known the jerk was going to be late, he would have stopped by Allen's lab instead of sitting on his butt here.

The room could have been a Hollywood set for a billionaire's office. Fresh flowers sat in a crystal vase on the teak sidebar next to a fancy coffee machine. Floral and caffeine scents mixed with the odor of leather oozing from the chairs. Quite a contrast with the beat-up furnishings in the criminology department's conference room. Someone had spent real money here.

His phone buzzed, and he snatched it from his pocket, hoping it might be Allen. The caller ID showed the Chief's name and Sam slumped. What the fuck did *he* want? "Sondergard here. What can I do for you, Chief?"

"Where you at, boy?"

"I'm at the Canine Research Facility at Browning, following up on a lead."

"You do something to set them eggheads off? I got a call from their head of security, Watson. The SOBs claiming jurisdiction over these bodies. That could screw up our whole plan."

That must be Dr. Mondrian's work. Maybe Sam would get the help he needed. "What plan is that, sir?"

"I told you. These bodies ain't got nothing to do with the good folks of Hollenbeck. They's outsiders, come here to make trouble." He huffed for a moment, and then continued. "Anyways, the damned college owns the land them bodies was on, so they're claiming that makes it their case. I ain't going to have no state po-lice sticking their snouts into what we do, you hear me?"

Sam closed his eyes. "What do you want me to do, sir?"

"You just do like I tell you. I already cut us a deal. This Watson guy's agreed to cooperate with our investigation instead of calling in the state. He's going assign one of his rent-a-cops, someone named Johansson, to work with you."

Brad Johansson was in Sam's criminal law class this fall. "I know him. I'll give him a call."

"You do that. And get this damned thing wrapped up as soon as you can. I tell you it's drugs is what's behind this. Big city gangs coming to our little town and defiling our youth. I'll have your ass if you fuck this up, boy."

"I'm doing my best, sir." *Asshole. I'll follow wherever the evidence leads.*

"See that you do. Keep them reports coming. Not today, though. I got meetings with the mayor and some of his friends. Dinner tonight, too, so don't bother me. Just send me an email."

"Yes, sir." He looked at his phone. The Chief had already broken the connection.

Where the fuck was Sarnok? Sam stood. If he can't be on time, then screw him. Allen's lab wasn't more than a five minute walk.

Before he could take a step toward the door, it opened and a heavy-set man puttered into the room. A fringe of hair sprouted around his head and face like steel wool halo, and his nervous eyes avoided looking Sam. "You must be Detective — Sondheim, is it?" He extended his hand and a grin fluttered across his features.

"Sondergard. Detective Sergeant Sam Sondergard." He held up the badge that hung from a strap at his neck. "You're Dr. Sarnok?" He wasn't at all like Allen had described him, from his flabby handshake to his nervous manner.

"Oh my, no. I'm Seth Harzig, the staff veterinarian. Dr. Sarnok will join us in a few minutes. His meeting with General — well, his meeting ran over. He asked me to attend to your needs in the meantime."

"His assistant, Ms. Eberhard, made a special point of telling me to be prompt," Sam snapped.

"The dragon lady? She was just throwing her weight around. Sarnok's always late. Makes him feel important." He strolled to the sidebar and raised an eyebrow at Sam. "Would you like coffee? This gizmo grinds the beans and serves it one cup at a time."

What Sam wanted was for the fucking interview to start on time. He wanted to know Allen was safe. He wanted the Chief not to be an asshole.

He clenched his jaws. *Control. None of that's this guy's fault.* "Sure. Thank you. When will Dr. Sarnok be here?"

"Soon, soon. I'm sure. Cream and sugar?"

"I'll fix mine, thank you." Sam fiddled with his coffee and controlled his breathing. "Tell me what you do here, Dr. Harzig."

"This and that." He shrugged and flopped into one of the leather desk chairs, and he blew on his coffee. "The law requires research facilities that use animals have a staff veterinarian. I do wellness checks on the specimens, provide care. The usual."

Sam pulled out his notebook. "Can you tell me what they do at this facility? I know it involves dogs."

Harzig slouched back and rested his sneaker-clad feet on one of the chairs. "Sure. It's an Army project. We're developing dogs for search-and-rescue missions in combat. The dogs can go places soldiers can't."

"You're training dogs for combat? Isn't that dangerous?" Sam pretended to take notes. Nothing new here. He already knew the broad outlines from Allen, but Harzig might let something slip Allen didn't know.

"No, no. These dogs aren't fighters. They're trained to *point*. All their conditioning is to search out a target. We've reinforced their natural instincts with a touch of genetic engineering. That's what makes dogs a perfect subject for this kind of thing. Their genome is so malleable."

"Genetically engineered dogs don't sound so safe to me. I've heard rumors."

Seth's eye's flicked to the left, then down. "Nonsense. We had an accident in the lab three years ago. A graduate student failed to follow protocols. The animals involved were all destroyed."

Sam jotted *he's lying* next to his notes. "Why destroy the animals if the student was at fault?"

"Precaution, I assure you. That was before Dr. Sarnok had external funding, and we could scarcely afford the expense, but we erred on the side of safety."

For sure, he's covering something up. Maybe Otis's wife Lizzie could help. Time to change the subject. "Talk to me about the funding." He gestured at the room. "The Army pays for all of this?"

"Well, the building was ARRA funding, back after the stock market crash. But yeah, they fund the research. It'll be worth it, too. Our dogs will save lives."

"What will they do?" Allen's explanations had gone off the deep end of canine psychology, operant training, and linguistics.

"It's simple, really. They have enhanced intelligence. That's the genetic engineering piece. We can give them detailed instructions, since they understand thousands of words. Grammar and syntax, too, which is connected with independent problem solving. We give them a target, set them loose in a chaotic urban environment, and they sniff out the target. Dogs have an incredible sense of smell, you know."

"Then what? They find the target and they bark?"

Harzig chuckled. "Detective, you have an ironic sense of humor. They wear a collar with a GPS chip and a short-range radio transmitter. When they make contact with the target, they nip at a switch that's surgically embedded in their forepaws. It sends a wireless signal to the collar and then to the dog's handler."

"That sounds needlessly complicated. Why not just hang a cell phone around the dog's neck?"

Seth rolled his eyes. "Like Anwar Province has working cell phone towers. Or post-Katrina New Orleans, for that matter. Plus, the idea is to use this for anti-terrorist operations-- the dog's under cover. This way, the bad guys just see a dog, not a secret agent using a cell phone."

The conference room door opened, and Sam turned to face a smiling man in a creased, white lab coat and a tailored suit. He could have been Robert Redford, except he'd aged better and was still good looking.

"Good morning, Detective. I see Dr. Harzig's been leaking our secrets again. I'm Dr. Sarnok. So sorry to have kept you waiting." His indifferent tone made it clear he wasn't at all sorry. He didn't offer to shake hands.

Sam stood, and Sarnok's eyes bore into him, sending a chill down his spine. He'd seen eyes like those before, in a man who'd slit the throat of his business partner and dissolved the body in acid. Allen was smart to distrust him. If only he was smart about other things. He swallowed back his anger and introduced himself. "Sam Sondergard, sir. Dr. Harzig has been most helpful."

"I'm sure. Seth, be a good fellow and fix me some coffee, will you? Cream and light on the sugar, please." He waved at the table while taking a seat. "Please sit, Detective. How may I help you?" He glanced at his watch. "I can give you ten minutes."

You can give me as much time as I need asshole. Sam reached into his pocket, pulled out the evidence bag with the tag Otis had found, and slid it across the table. "Do you recognize this?" He had to raise his voice over the rasp of grinding coffee.

Irritation flicked across Sarnok's features as he glanced at the bag, then his eyebrows lifted, and his eyes widened a few millimeters. "Where did you obtain this? It's lab property."

"It was buried in the grasp of a severed human hand."

Seth slopped coffee onto the carpet as he served Sarnok. "A severed hand? This must be about those bodies at Dr. Eckhorn's habitat." He snatched the evidence bag from the table. "This is from a second generation animal. All of those were destroyed, along with their tags, three years ago." His fingers trembled, and his voice had the slightest quaver.

Sam stayed focused on Sarnok. "Well, Doctor? If this is lab property, how did it wind up in my murder victim's hand?"

Sarnok flipped dismissive fingers at him. "I really have no idea. Disposition of the badges and retired animals is the responsibility of the staff veterinarian, Dr. Harzig. I'm sure our accountant, Mrs. Bateman, has the required records if you want to examine them."

This stank like yesterday's dog shit. Why did Sarnok make sure Harzig was the one here in the conference room while Sam waited? It had to be some kind of setup. "I do want to examine those records, sir. But right now, I'm asking you. What can you tell me about the dog that wore that tag?"

Sarnok sniffed. "Really, is that important? Let me see it, please." He held the bag between his thumb and forefinger and peered at the contents. "This was from specimen 2.1, a second generation CHIP prototype. A male, as I recall. It tested high on the intelligence scale, but turned out to be less susceptible to conditioning than we'd hoped. We moved on to more refined designs."

Sam leaned forward. "Is this the animal who attacked the graduate student?"

Sarnok's eyes narrowed, and he gave Harzig a sideways glance. "That was a training accident, not an attack. I'd have to check the records."

"So there was an attack. What was the name of the student? I'd like to talk to her."

"How should I know? She dropped out, and she wasn't that strong academically anyway. I told you. Mrs. Bateman has the records."

The jerk wouldn't take responsibility for anything. "Look, this is a murder investigation. Multiple murders. We have reason to believe there's a killer out there, probably with a vicious dog. I need you to stop evading my questions and give me answers."

"I have been cooperating, *Detective.* I find your tone bordering on harassment. I'll have you know the mayor is a good friend of mine. In fact, I'm meeting with him this afternoon." He stood. "In the meantime, why don't you talk to Dr. Harzig? Or one of my graduate students. Mr. LaClerc, for example. He's not hopelessly stupid."

Harzig looked up at Allen's name. "He's not here. He didn't come in this morning."

The hairs on the back of Sam's neck prickled. He didn't go home last night, and now he didn't come to work this morning. "He's missing?" *God, tell me he's not missing.*

Sarnok shrugged. "He probably just overslept."

Harzig shook his head. "I don't think so. We spoke yesterday, and he was definitely planning on coming in this morning. He was working on a term paper that's due today, so I checked with Dr. Eckhorn. She said he didn't come to class, either."

Fuck, fuck, fuck. That sealed it. Sam pulled out his cell phone. While he called Allen, he asked, "Is it like him to not come in?"

Harzig shook his head. "Not Allen. He's obsessive about the lab, and Teena. She's the subject of his dissertation."

"Really, Dr. Harzig," Sarnok interjected. "It's a research specimen, not a pet. Call it by its proper designation, 13.5."

Allen's phone again went to voice mail. Sam's fingers trembled as put it back in his pocket. *What to do?* He turned to Harzig. "When did you last speak to him?"

"Last night. Maybe about six or so. It was raining, and I offered him a ride, but he turned me down. I saw him crossing the intramural field about ten minutes later."

No ride. After all my warnings, he still was out alone walking. "Where was he headed?"

"Home, I think he said. What's this about?"

Walking through the warehouse district, then. Where we found the first body, God help him. "I told you. I have reason to believe there's a serial killer on the loose. If I'm right, he's targeting young men like Allen. I mean, Mr. LeClerc." Sam tried not to think of Eric Bell's mutilated body. His stomach roiled and he swallowed saliva.

Harzig's eyes grew to billiard ball size. "Shit. A *serial* killer here in Hollenbeck?"

Sarnok's tone turned prim. "Really, Detective, you're over-reacting. The Chief personally told me this whole dead body thing was drug related and had nothing to do with our community. Mr. LeClerc is just a silly, irresponsible graduate student who cut class and blew off his job."

Sam's face burned. He clenched his fists and shouted, "He's a human being, you arrogant ass wipe. He's missing.

No one's spoken to him or seen him for over twelve hours. I've got to find him."

"How dare you — " Sarnok stopped and leaned forward. "You're going to conduct a search, you say? Perhaps I can help. We need a field test." His eyes glowed.

Harzig's head snapped around to face Sarnok. "You mean use one of the dogs? I don't care what the Army says, they're not ready."

Sarnok waved him off and kept his attention on Sam. "I'll be the sole judge of that. Detective, I'm certain that our prototype 13.5 can locate Mr. LeClerc, wherever he is. I'd be glad to offer the project's assistance in your search."

Sam rubbed his eyes and tried to think. No way Chief Hartman would let him put any resources toward finding Allen. He'd barely been gone twelve hours, and nothing concrete connected him to the murder investigation. Given the Chief's attitude toward gay people, it'd be even worse if Sam revealed their relationship. The state police might help, but not in time to do any good. If he was going to find Allen, he was pretty much on his own.

He locked eyes with Sarnok. "I accept your offer. When can we get started?"

Chapter 15

1148, Wednesday, October 31

The first thing Allen noticed was pain. Pain and pressure. His head throbbed. It pulsed in cadence with each heartbeat. He was sure blood was inflating and deflating his brain like a balloon, pressing it against his skull and then relenting.

Brains couldn't explode, could they?

A buzz droned in his ears. When had that started? Underneath, sometimes audible, sometimes, not, music swelled in a slow cycle of crescendos and diminuendos. He could almost make out the song. *Nights in White Satin,* that was it. He'd played it at dinner with Sam.

Sam. There was something he needed to tell him, but he couldn't remember what.

What was that awful smell? It reminded him of Aunt Edna. No. Not Edna. Her thirteen cats. Poor Edna. She was too feeble to care for herself. Or her cats. Or their litter boxes. *Why was he with Edna? She lived in Dubuque, not Hollenbeck.*

No, wait. Edna was dead. He'd gone to her funeral when he was a junior in high school. If he was with Edna, then he was dead. That would explain a lot.

Would he still hurt if he was dead?

God, the stink was unbearable. If only he could breathe through his mouth, but it wouldn't open.

Dark. It's dark as a cave. If he was in hell, wouldn't there be fire? Let there be light. Nope. Not god. It's still dark.

Oh. His eyes were closed. He concentrated. The lids wouldn't open. They couldn't be glued shut, could they?

Shit. His nose itched. His arms wouldn't move to scratch it. The muscles tensed, but they were stuck, like his eyelids. He curled his lip and twisted his facial muscles. Damn it. Don't sneeze. It's going to hurt if you sneeze.

A spasm gripped him when it came. The back of his head slammed against something hard, and the pain soared from ache to fire.

His right eye burst open, and furious blinks fought against the sudden glare. Tears flowed down his cheeks. He squeezed his eye shut to clear it of the crusty gunk that clung to his eyelashes and the edges of his eyelid. His left eye came unstuck. Chromatic halos surrounded the meaningless lumps of light and dark all around him. Everything glowed like ill-formed, underwater pearls.

Snot clogged his nose and drooled down his upper lip. For some reason, he couldn't breathe through his mouth. He pulled with his jaws. Nothing. It was stuck, like his eyes had been and his arms and legs still were. He sniffled to try to clear his nose and sneezed again. Shit. He expanded his nostrils and gulped in air. That was better. The stink wasn't as bad, either. Maybe there was an upside to snot in his nose.

From his position and the pressure on his butt and his back, he could tell he was in a chair. He could wiggle arms and elbows, but not ankles and wrists. He squeezed his eyes shut again and blinked them clear. *Aha.* Duct tape bound his wrists to the arms of his chair. Probably his wrists, too. He wriggled his mouth. Probably tape there, too. That would explain why it wouldn't open.

Shit. He was fucking naked. *What was going on?* He shook his head, and pain pulsed. The Moody Blues continued to croon, a surreal soundtrack to the horror movie his life had become.

Even the fucking chair could have come from a Wes Craven nightmare. With its combination of a rusted metal frame and cracked leather padding, it could have been a barber chair for *Sweeney Todd.* Or for the sadists in *Hostel.*

Footsteps shuffled on his right, and he twisted his gaze in that direction. An old man with scraggly, gray hair that hung in greasy ropes to his collar hunkered in the doorway. His stench reached across the room and gagged Allen. He wore grimy blue jeans and a flannel shirt that hung on his frame like clothes on a scarecrow. He had a chicken leg in one fist and was chewing with his mouth open. A chunk of meat ejected itself from his mouth and landed on the floor.

"Well, lookie there. You awake, my precious?" The man's voice caressed his ears like velvet on tender flesh.

Teena scampered into the room, and Allen's heart leaped. But this dog's fur had iron-gray flecks, not silver. Its ear flopped, where Teena had her CHIP tag. Oh, and it was male. Not Teena. It gobbled up the scrap of chicken from the floor, looked up, and wagged its tail.

Then Allen remembered seeing the dog on the street and making the same mistake. He wasn't Teena, he was Spot. Worse, he was a second generation CHIP. Allen remembered talking to the old man, getting in his van. How did he end up here?

Where was here, anyway? The room came to sudden focus. Next to the wall, a naked man lay supine, strapped to a rusty hospital stretcher. His eyes were closed and his muscles flaccid. He must be unconscious. Or dead. *Dear god, please don't let him be dead.*

Shapeless globs floated in jars stacked on shelves under a cracked window. Knives, meat hooks, and other horrible *sharp* things rested on a metal table next to the other captive. Allen leaned forward and narrowed his eyes. Brown puddles of congealed glop pooled on the metal surface. That had to be dried blood.

Motion from the jars drew his attention back in their direction. A random eddy disturbed the contents of one, and an eyeball rotated to stare at him, trailing an optic nerve like a worm sucking at it.

Allen's stomach roiled. He couldn't help himself. Vomit burned his throat. With nowhere else to go, it jetted out his nose and down his front.

He remembered what he needed to tell Sam. He'd been right to worry about the serial killer.

How could Allen have been so stupid?

The man, what was his name? Charley? No, Charley worked at the Pride Center. Bobby, that was it. Bobby danced in slow circles to the music, rotating toward the table and the still body on the stretcher. His soothing voice hummed in off-key dissonance with the recording. He paused at the table and picked up a scalpel.

Allen's heart chilled. He needed to scream, he had to scream, but he had no mouth. Just a duct-taped hole that wouldn't open.

A sly grin split Bobby's face and he cast a sidelong glance at Allen. "Watch, my precious. You're going to enjoy this." His dulcet tone promised a communion of souls. But his eyes were death, cold and implacable.

Allen's spine turned to ice, his gut to a black hole of despair. He had no doubt this was hell, and that it was filled with pain.

Bobby reached out and the scalpel gleamed in a beam of sunlight. He used his fingers to measure the spot, and then lowered the blade to the chest of the man on the stretcher. Just a touch. So slight. So delicate.

A stream of thick, Merlot-dark blood bathed the man's naked torso. Random rivulets dribbled down his side and puddled on the floor. Despite the duct tape around his mouth, he managed to release a stuttering sequence of anguished shrieks. His head thrashed back and forth. The muscles on his body rippled, exposing artery and sinew.

He was alive after all.

Maybe he'd be better off dead.

Spot trotted closer, his eyes glowing. He lowered his head and lapped at the crimson fluid that leaked to the floor.

Bobby leaned over and stroked his captive's brow. "My darling, don't worry. That was just a little love bite for you. Old Bobby, he'll take care of you. You're my precious." He pressed a filthy rag against the incision he'd just made under the man's nipple. "Bobby won't let you die. It's not our time, yours and mine. Soon, but not yet."

The victim's eyes bulged and rolled to stare at Allen. They sent a voiceless plea for rescue, or maybe release.

Allen gasped. He recognized Pete, the ROTC guy from the Tool Box a couple of weeks ago. Shit. How did *he* wind up here? No one deserved this. Allen tried to shout for Bobby to stop, but all the duct tape let him emit were grunts. His muffled cries scorched his throat. The tape binding him bit into his skin. A bead of blood trickled from his right wrist onto the arm of his chair, leaving a crimson trail. He must have cut himself on the exposed metal.

Bobby gave him that *look* again, and a tender, terrifying smile played with his features. "Don't fret, my love. I haven't forgotten you. First, you get to watch me and my angel here play. After," he licked his lips. "After, then we'll have *our* fun."

Allen closed his eyes. He sucked air through his nose. Panic jack-hammered his body. Shudders, deep and violent, wracked his body. He wasn't ready to die. Not yet.

Bobby's face appeared next to Allen's, as sudden as if he'd teleported. The stench of decay and stale beer fouled the air.

Bobby whispered, "My precious." He stroked Allen's hair. "Think how *alive* you are at this instant. That's my *gift* to you, and yours to me. We'll never be as alive, either of us, as we are in the moments we share."

Fuck, fuck, fuck. He's bat shit crazy. Make it *stop.* Make him *go away.* The music had changed. Think about that. Think about anything but Bobby and his madness. What was playing? Another oldie. The Drifters? *This Magic Moment.* That was it.

Bobby kissed his ear, his breath hot against Allen's skin. He murmured, "It will be *our* magic moment. To the end of time. Our window to eternity."

Allen tossed his head and recoiled. Insanity threatened to boil his mind to nothingness. *Make him go away. Please, please, please.*

Bobby chuckled. "What's that my love? Please, you say? You're begging already? Time enough for that later." Still chuckling, he shuffled from the room.

Spot rested on his haunches, his tail thumping on the floor. He lay down and held something with his forepaws. When he started to gnaw on it, Allen realized it was a bone. A strange, long, bone, with gristle and green-tinged muscle. Disgusting.

Sunlight slanted through the window. A siren sounded in the distance before fading to oblivion. A siren. Police. What would happen to Sam? They could have had a life together, been happy, like real people. Why did Allen get so mad at him, instead of telling him how he felt? His chin quivered under the tape and tears leaked from his eyes.

The music changed again. Another oldie. Roy Orbison, this time. *Crying.*

Allen stiffened his back. *Stop it. Don't cry. Plan. Use your wits. Get out of this. Somehow.* He had to. For Pete. For Sam.

For himself.

Chapter 16

1448, Wednesday, October 31

Sam checked his phone for what seemed like the thousandth time. No voice mail. No texts. He needed to *do* something. Instead, Sarnok had him wasting time in this damned electronics lab while they screwed around with their tech. Maybe Harzig was right, and they weren't ready.

On the other side of the room, Sarnok hovered over a graduate student. Sweat gleamed on her brow, and her lips moved as she read code from the three monitors arrayed on her desk.

The lab was a prime candidate for an episode of *Hoarders.* Circuit boards, old keyboards, and dark CRTs jammed the shelves lining the walls. Stacks of paper covered with computer code and yet more computer junk cluttered the workbench in the middle of the room.

Harzig slouched on a conference room chair in one corner, his eyes closed and chin slumped against his chest. How could the man nap at a time like this?

Enough, already. "Timing is everything in missing person cases, Dr. Sarnok. How much longer will you be?"

Sarnok's eyebrows lifted. "We'll be ready when we're ready, Detective. It's a mistake to rush these things." He put a hand on the graduate student's shoulder and squeezed. "Tell the Detective, Ms. Gomez. You're doing your best."

She flinched at his touch and cast a harried look at Sam. "If I'd *known* we were going to run a test today, I wouldn't have started this update on the collar's OS. It'll be another fifteen minutes." She looked back at the screen and flicked a strand of hair from her face. "Make that twenty. I'm going as fast as I can."

"You see, Detective?" Sarnok's tone managed to be smug and condescending at the same time. "She's doing her *best*." He squeezed her shoulder again, and she cringed.

Harzig grunted to his feet. "We're just distracting them, Detective. I could use a smoke. You want to join me?"

"I quit." Sam wasn't going anywhere.

"Good for you. I quit at least once a week." Harzig proceeded to the door where he paused, right behind Sarnok and the graduate student. "Join me. It'll get us out of their hair. I'll smoke two cigarettes. That's fourteen minutes. Fifteen, tops. We can talk about Allen. Or movies. Or I can brief you on the damned technology. It'll give you something to do instead of sitting here fidgeting."

Sarnok nodded. "Good idea. Let Dr. Harzig brief you. Really, your presence here is quite distracting."

Sam glared at him. *Why let that asshole tell him what to do?*

Behind Sarnok, Harzig tossed his head backwards and rolled his eyes in an exaggerated gesture. He then gave his boss the finger with both hands.

Sam's mouth twitched. Maybe Harzig was right. "Fifteen minutes. We'll be back." He let Harzig lead him away.

Harzig stayed silent until they turned down a side corridor. "Don't let him get to you. He's really a brilliant scientist."

"He's a first class prick, that's what he is." He followed Harzig outside to a park bench nestled under a willow tree. A light breeze rustled through the low-hanging branches.

"He's that, too." Harzig lit a cigarette and exhaled a cloud of blue smoke. He offered the pack to Sam. "Sure you don't want one?"

Virginia Slim menthols. Was he an old queen or what? Sam stared at the open pack and bit his lip. Just one wouldn't hurt, and it might take some of the edge off. He accepted the offer and let Harzig light it for him. The first long drag rasped and cooled his throat at the same time. He held it, and in seconds, tension oozed from his muscles. "I'd forgotten. Thanks. It does help."

Harzig nodded. "Keep taking deep puffs. That enhances the nicotine's release of beta-endorphins." He took another drag. "Endogenous morphine. That's what makes having a cigarette so *satisfying.*"

Shit. Two drags and he was already buzzed. At least he no longer felt an urgent need to punch someone out. He'd pay for this later, when his mouth tasted like shit. Ashtray mouth, Allen called it. He wouldn't want to kiss. Assuming Sam found him. Assuming he was alive. Assuming any of this worked. He turned a glum eye on Harzig. "Talk to me, will you? Can that dog really find Allen?"

"I'm not the expert. Allen thought she was ready for trials. I can tell you that. Sarnok does, too, and he should know."

Well, if Allen thought it would work, that was something. "But you said you didn't think she was ready."

"I'm just a vet, not a scientist. Teena's only been in simulations, not in the real world. No one knows what she'll make of what she finds out there. Shit, it's Halloween. What'll she think about some kid dressed like a zombie?"

"I can't wrap my brain about that--a thinking dog. I mean, dogs can't think, can they Dr. Harzig?"

"Seth. Call me Seth." He patted the bench. "Sit. Use this chance to relax, so you'll be fresh later."

Sam hesitated, and then perched on the opposite end from Seth. "I'm Sam, by the way."

"Sam, I don't know if she can think or not. But she can understand words, and grammar, too. They've even set up a kind of object-oriented sign language for her using squeeze toys. I've seen her ask for things. Bacon, for example. If you try to give her turkey, she'll shake her head no and push the bacon toy back at you."

That meshed with what Allen said. He paused for another drag. "If she's so smart, then why all the tech? Why can't they just, you know, release the hounds?"

Seth chuckled. "Like a movie. I know. It's more complex than that. Teena's smart, and she'll understand the mission. She'll improvise and respond to her environment. She can go places you can't. Follow her nose, so to speak." He stared at the glowing coal of his cig. "That tiny computer in her collar, it's kind of like an iWatch. It's got a GPS chip, and a radio that we can ping from the control center here. That way we'll always know where she is."

"So I have to hang around here, doing nothing while she searches?"

"No, that's my job." He rubbed his belly. "I'm suited to hanging around. We'll give you a transponder of your own, but yours will receive the signal from here instead of sending. It also has a GPS display that relays from here where she's at. Both signals are encrypted."

"So I can trail her, but don't have to keep her in sight?" Sam sucked in another deep drag. *Shit, it was three quarters gone already*.

"Ex*act*-a-mundo. She can search without distractions, and without alerting the bad guys. You can relax in your squad car, following along."

"I won't be in a squad car." *Won't be relaxing, either*. Sam took a final draw and crushed the butt against the sole of his sneaker. He field-stripped it while considering strategy. *Can't risk backup*. If the Chief found out about this search,

136

he'd forbid it as a waste of time. It went against all Sam's training, but it didn't matter. He had to find Allen, and that meant going in alone. "I'll be driving my personal Honda."

Seth shrugged. "Whatever. In the field, the soldiers might be on foot, or a motorcycle, or a pogo stick for all I know. The point is, you'll get a signal when she finds him and can charge in to the rescue." He chain-smoked a new cigarette.

"Right. You covered that. She bites her foot or something." Sam looked at the Virginia Slims with longing.

"That's it." Seth slipped a book of matches into the cellophane surrounding the pack and handed it to him. "Here. Keep it. You look like you need them more than I do."

Sam hesitated and then accepted. "Maybe you're right." He lit another cigarette. One more and they'd go back inside. He sat, elbows on his knees, and tried to visualize his tactics after Teena found Allen.

****

Teena squatted on her haunches and twitched her nose. The smells in this place were new, and so *interesting.* She resisted the urge to bury herself inside the room-with-wheels and sniff out all the exotic odors that wafted from its open door. DoctorSarnok's command to *stay* had been clear. She was a *good*dog. She always did what she was told.

DoctorSarnok and DoctorHarzig chattered about something, but Teena didn't know all the words. If Allen had been here, *he* would have used words Teena understood. She missed Allen.

Allen's new friend Sam leaned against a wall all hunched into himself. She recognized his scent first, kind of musky and mixed with the leather of his jacket. There was an undercurrent of Allen, too. Teena liked that. Something new overlaid all that, something that wasn't there before. Kind of smokey, like DoctorHarzig.

But most of all Sam smelled like fear. Teena wanted to lick his hand and make him feel better. Her tail thumped on the floor, and she almost trotted over to him before she remembered. She needed to "*stay*," like DoctorSarnok had said.

She was a *good*dog. Allen always told her that, so it must be true.

DoctorSarnok stomped up to her and shouted, "Thirteen. Listen to me."

He always called her 'Thirteen,' just like he always called Allen 'MisterLeClerc.' He was so funny. Maybe he couldn't remember the right names for people. Teena nodded her head so he would know she was listening. His voice hurt her ears.

"Mr. LeClerc is in danger. You need to *find* Mr. Leclerc." He shoved a lab coat under her nose.

Teena touched her nose to the coat so DoctorSarnok would know she smelled it, even though she didn't need to sniff it. Allen's scent was strong in the cloth. She nodded her head. Find Allen. They played that game a lot. It was fun.

Sarnok continued to yell at her. "You must concentrate. Your mission is to *find* him. He's hidden away, and you must *trail* his scent and *find* him. Do you understand?"

She'd already told him that, but she nodded again anyway. DoctorSarnok always repeated himself. He must not be good at remembering things. Not like Teena. She always remembered things.

"When you find him, send the *signal*." DoctorSarnok scowled at her. "Show me how you send the *signal*."

Teena raised her leg and nipped at her right paw. Silly DoctorSarnok. He must have forgotten how she sent the signal. Teena was a smart dog. She never forgot.

"Good dog. After you *send* the signal, *hide*. If Allen moves, *follow*, but continue to *hide*. Do not approach him. Do you understand?"

Teena nodded her head. If she found Allen, why couldn't she nuzzle him? Allen was always glad to see her. He had treats, too. She loved him even when he didn't have treats. But if DoctorSarnok said to *hide*, Teena would hide. She was a *good*dog.

DoctorSarnok grabbed her muzzle and stared into her eyes. She hated it when he did that. He squawked, "Thirteen. *Trail. Find. Signal. Hide.* Do you understand?"

For sure DoctorSarnok had bad memory. Teena just told him she understood. She nodded again and tried to lick his hand. Poor DoctorSarnok, not able to remember things like Teena.

He snatched his hand back and reached into his pocket.

Teena perked her ears, but instead of a treat he pulled out a white cloth and wiped his hands. It smelled like flowers. Did DoctorSarnok keep flowers in his pocket? Teena wanted to look. No, wait. She needed to *stay*. She was a *good*dog.

DoctorHarzig knelt next to her and put a collar around her neck. He ruffled her ears and whispered, "That's a good dog, Teena. Allen's depending on you. We all are."

That meant Allen needed her to do what DoctorSarnok said. Teena nodded her head. They could depend on her. She was a gooddog. The *best*dog. It must be true. Allen said so.

Besides, Teena loved playing the find-Allen game. Maybe he would have a treat for her after it was over.

Chapter 17

1632, Wednesday, October 31

Teena lay with her head on her paws and let the vibration of the room-on-wheels purr against her tummy. Allen always made it fun when he took her for a ride in a room-with-wheels. He'd let her hang out the window where the wind blew in her ears and the smells sped through the air. But DoctorSarnok pointed to the back and told her to *sit*. She was a gooddog. She sat.

DoctorHarzig sat in front, sucking on a not-quite-burning white tube. *Interesting* smells trailed from it and into Teena's nose. Stinky, but interesting. DoctorHarzig inhaled from the tube, the end glowed red, and then a cloud of smoke puffed from his lips. Teena inhaled, too, but it was just stinky. Maybe DoctorHarzig liked stinky.

DoctorSarnok said, "Put that damned thing out." His voice was angry.

The room-on-wheels swerved and Teena's tail thumped on the floor. Moving rooms were scary. Fun-scary, not hurt-scary.

DoctorHarzig pushed the tube into a box built into the room. "Happy now?" His voice was angry, but in a different way from DoctorSarnok. Teena knew from the slope of his shoulders and his smell that he was afraid as well as mad. Maybe he was in DoctorSarnok's pack and he was afraid DoctorSarnok would bite him. Teena was in Allen's pack. She was glad she wasn't in DoctorSarnok's pack.

The room-on-wheels jerked and stopped moving. The two humans got out and the side door next to Teena slid open with a screech. She lifted her head and probed with her nose. So many new smells. Old, familiar ones, too. Like pizza. Allen sometimes let her eat pizza. It was yummy. Lots and lots of human smells, too. Tens and tens of them, more than she'd ever sensed before. Rain smells, concrete smells, earth smells.

There were lots and lots of the stinky smells that the rooms-with-wheels made, too. Those cooled her nostrils and tickled at the same time. Each was different, as though every room-with-wheels were a different creature. The rabbits that she sometimes sniffed when Allen let her play outside all smelled different, too.

DoctorSarnok yelled, "Thirteen. Come here. *Sit.*" He pointed to his feet.

Teena hopped onto the concrete and blinked against the sunlight. Her heart thumped in her chest. Something was going to happen. She knew it. She sat next to DoctorSarnok and waited.

He held Allen's coat against her nose. "Smell this. It belongs to Allen."

Teena sniffed, even though she done it before, not long ago. DoctorSarnok had a bad memory, not at all like Teena. She nodded to help him remember.

"*Trail* the scent. *Find* Allen. When you find him, send the *signal*. Then *hide*. Do you understand, Thirteen?"

Teena sat on her haunches, stared at DoctorSarnok, and nodded. Her tail swept across the pavement.

Another room-on-wheels rolled next to them, and Sam got out. She inhaled his scent. Smoke, like DoctorHarzig. Maybe he liked stinky, too? She sniffed again and whimpered. Sam was *afraid*, very afraid. She wanted to nuzzle his hand, but DoctorSarnok said to *sit*. She was a gooddog.

DoctorSarnok gripped her muzzle and tipped her head up. Saliva puddled in her mouth, and she fought the urge to nip at him. Allen wouldn't like it if she did that.

He shouted at her. "*Trail, find, signal, hide*. Show me you understand."

Why was DoctorSarnok so angry? She nodded her head again. Of course she understood. She'd just told him. Poor DoctorSarnok.

He released her and pointed. "Go. Start. Find him."

Teena nodded again and lowered her nose to the concrete, casting back and forth. There it was. Allen's scent! So faint, so very faint, she could barely pick it out. Her heart beat faster, and she raced after it, in the direction DoctorSarnok pointed.

"Thirteen. Stop." DoctorSarnok sounded even angrier.

Teena stopped and looked to him for instructions.

"Not *that* way, you idiot mutt. That's back toward the Zoology building. That's where he came from." He pointed at a clear grassy area. "*That* way. Follow the trail that way."

Teena yipped, excitement burning in her veins. That way, this way, any way. She was a gooddog. The best. She loved the find-Allen game. It was fun. She could follow instructions.

The trail was faint, but she was smart. Sometimes the trail ended at mud puddles, but Teena knew Allen couldn't disappear. She sniffed around and around until she picked him up again. Allen was *good* at this game, but Teena was better. She always won. Afterwards, when she found him, Allen always ruffled her ears, gave her a treat, and called her a *good*dog.

Allen must have stopped at the far side of the flat, grassy place. His scent grew stronger, and wandered in a little circle.

Some sadness leaked in, too, along with the strong odor of human males sweating. Teena shivered. When Allen was sad, she was, too. The trail moved on, over a strange hill with metal bars running away in both directions. She almost lost him there, but she caught a whiff from the other side of a fence.

She cast back and forth and found an opening. On the other side, his scent was even stronger. This place was all grassy, too, with a subtle odor of decay. Stones stood in long rows. Allen's path wove in and out, as though always keeping to one side of the stones. Humans did such strange things. Even Allen.

She paused at the top of a hill. It smelled bad. She sniffed all around the bottom. Little plastic bubbles that smelled like the gloves Trish wore. Except these were filled with slimy human smells. *Interesting*. But that wasn't what smelled bad. That was just human stink.

Teena sniffed again, and this time the odor of dog pee made her bark. She sniffled and shivered. A relative had peed here. It was a male. Was it maybe Deuce? Was he looking for Allen, too? Sometimes they played a game about who would find Allen first. She nosed at the leaves and inhaled. No. Not Deuce. A relative, but not from her litter. There was wrongness in this dog. His smell carried danger. Death.

Teena howled. Bad smell. This was a *bad*dog. A *very* baddog.

Then she shuddered and remembered her mission. Find Allen. She was a good dog. She ignored the bad dog smell and sought out her friend. Yes, there he was, heading away from the bad dog smell. Good.

She followed Allen's scent to a metal fence, then through to the other side. His smell was strong now, with not so many distractions. She recognized a *sidewalk* and a *street* from the games she and Allen played. *Streets* were where rooms-on-wheels went. They could run over Teena and hurt her, so she looked both ways before crossing, the way Allen taught her. No rooms-on-wheels. She trotted to the *sidewalk* on the other side.

Allen's trail continued. The bad dog smell was here, too. Worry made Teena run. The bad dog would hurt Allen if he could. She was sure of it.

She skittered to a halt. Where did Allen's scent go? It just vanished. There weren't any puddles to sniff around. She circled back and picked it up again. This time she kept her nose to the ground.

There was Allen. He stopped and the bad dog smell was right there next to him. There was a bad people smell, too. A man. And a dead thing smell. A few feet later, all the smells vanished except a sneezy smell from a room-on-wheels.

Teena sniffed and sniffed. She re-traced the scents. She circled in wider and wider circuits. Nothing. No more Allen. No more baddog.

The only thing she picked up was a room-on-wheels. Its stinky-cool smell blossomed right where Allen's and bad dog's disappeared.

That must mean something.

Teena hunkered down, her head on her paws and thought.

Find Allen. She was a good dog. A *smart* dog. Allen told her so. Sometimes she had to figure out tricks to win the find-Allen game. Maybe this was like that.

She closed her eyes and tried to picture Allen and baddog together. Baddog growled and bit Allen's neck! No. That didn't happen. She could *smell* it if that happened. But baddog wanted to bite Allen, she was sure of that. Anger and death were in his scent.

Baddog wanted to hurt Allen, but he hadn't done it. Yet. Fear chilled Teena's belly worse than eating ice cream too fast. She could still see bad dog tearing Allen's flesh. Like it was happening right now. Her heart hammered, and she peed on the concrete. Just a little. Not what a good dog does.

Maybe this wasn't a game. Maybe DoctorSarnok sent baddog to hurt Allen. Maybe *that* was why Sam was so scared. Maybe Allen was in danger. Sam loved Allen, she could tell. His smell when they were together told her. Of course, that was why he was scared.

Teena would find Allen. No one would hurt him. Not *ever*. Not while Teena breathed.

Then in a flash she knew what happened to Allen's trail. It was so simple. Allen and baddog didn't just disappear. That couldn't happen. *They must have gotten in a room-on-wheels.* All Teena had to do was follow the scent of the room-on-wheels. It was right there where they'd vanished. It would be easy to trail. *Smart*dog.

With an excited woof, she scampered to her feet and picked up the trail.

****

Sam watched Teena bound off across the intramural field, despair clenching his throat. This couldn't actually work, could it?

Harzig touched his shoulder. "She'll find him. Don't worry."

"You really think so?"

"I do." Harzig hesitated. "Allen's been different lately. Happy. He told me he's seeing someone special."

Sam's face heated. "I don't — "

Harzig shook his head. "Shush. You don't have to say anything. I'm grateful to the person who turned on the light in Allen's soul. Whoever that is. Just know that I'll do whatever I can to help. I care for him, too."

Turned on the light in his soul. That was what Allen did for *Sam.* His throat tightened, and he gripped Harzig's hand. "Thanks." What else to say? "I mean it."

Harzig nodded, squeezed his hand, then his tone turned official. "You know how to use the relay?"

"Yeah. It's in my car."

"Okay then. Let me get back to the lab, where I'll monitor things." He scrawled on a business card. "Here are numbers for the lab and my cell phone. I've got yours already. Call me if you need anything."

"Got it."

Harzig grinned at him. "What are you waiting for? Go! It's going to be all right. You'll see."

Sam climbed in his car and sat while Harzig and Sarnok sped away.

The transponder rested on the seat beside him. It was pretty clunky, about the size of a bulky tablet computer. Instead of a cursor, a dog's head blinked on the GPS display marking Teena's position. Sam watched it meander around the intramural field and stop. He looked up. What was the damned dog up to? She sniffed all around a puddle of water, sat on her haunches and scratched behind her ear.

This was a super dog?

He glanced at his watch. It would be dark soon, and a heavy overcast hung over the campus. If it rained again, there wouldn't be any trail at all for Teena to follow, would there? Even the smartest dog on the planet couldn't follow nothing.

She was moving again. More aimless wandering, casting back and forth. Shit. She must have already lost the scent, and she was trying to re-find it. It had rained last night, too. Maybe there wasn't any scent left.

No, she was moving again, nose to the ground.

Now what's she doing at that tree, taking a leak?

146

Sam squirmed in his seat. How could he have been so stupid as to think this could possibly work? He glanced at his watch again. Twenty minutes wasted already, and the damned dog was just sitting licking her butt.

Fifteen minutes later, Sam was ready to call the Chief and try to convince him to launch a search. Anything was better than this. But Teena finally reached the artificial ravine that held the railroad tracks. Her pace suddenly became more purposeful, and she loped along before disappearing down the hill toward the tracks. He turned to the screen, and followed the too-cute-for-words doggie-cursor over the railroad tracks. He wondered if it was Allen's idea of a joke. It would be like him.

At least Teena was finally on the move.

The railroad tracks. Of course. Allen was walking home, and right into the arms of the killer. Shit. Why had Sam let him be so stupid? He should have insisted, even if it made Allen mad. He could have been more diplomatic, made him understand. Instead, they just fought.

Sam started his car and pulled out of the parking lot. He couldn't follow Teena's route, but he could circle a mile south and cross the tracks onto Jenkins Avenue. He'd pick her up from there. Good thing he had the GPS tracker to follow.

Sam sped through the late afternoon traffic, and then turned onto Wilson Avenue and the nearest railroad crossing. A dozen cars lined up in front of him, where a freight train lumbered across the street at about two miles an hour. Sam stretched his neck and spotted the end about fifteen tanker cars away.

Great. At this pace, the train would be clear in less than five minutes. The GPS showed the dog was still hanging around inside Eagles Cemetery. Plenty of time.

His phone buzzed. The caller ID read Chief Hartman. Fuck him. Sam tossed his phone onto the passenger seat and drummed his fingers on the steering wheel. A glance at the GPS tracker showed that Teena had left the cemetery and was on Jenkins. Shit. Hurry up, god damn it.

The train clanked to a stop. The damned thing creaked, moaned, and then *reversed direction.* Shit, shit, shit. How long was this going to take?

He gripped the GPS tracker in one hand and the steering wheel in the other. The doggie icon had stopped on Jenkins Avenue. What was up? Had she lost the scent?

The train groaned along at maybe fucking five miles an hour. The end disappeared among run-down warehouses, so there was no way to estimate how long this was going to take. Maybe he should circle another mile south and take *that* crossing. With traffic, that would take what? Fifteen minutes with luck, twenty without.

He checked the GPS again. The icon blinked off and on. Off and on. Off.

What the fuck? He tapped at the screen. Still no icon. Shit.

He fumbled with the card Harzig had given him. His fingers shook as he punched in the lab number. Control yourself. You've got to stay calm. Busy. Fuck. Fuck.

He pressed end, then tried Harzig's number. Voicemail. Shit. What the hell was going on?

Chapter 18

1738, Wednesday, October 31

Seth Harzig peered over Samantha Gomez's shoulder at her monitor. The doggie-shaped icon blinked on and off. "I wonder why she's stopped in the middle of the cemetery."

Samantha shrugged. "Who knows? She's a dog. Maybe she found a cute boy dog."

Seth's features relaxed into a grin. "Maybe. But she's trained to carry out her mission. I don't think even the Ryan Gosling of dogs would distract her."

"Oh, he's so *yesterday*, Dr. Harzig. Now Evan Peters-- he's dreamy."

Who the fuck was that? Seth must be completely out of it. Kids today. "Whose idea was the doggie icon?"

"Allen thought it up, but I did it. Cute, huh?"

"To cute for words." The icon blipped on and off, not moving. "Well, something's caught her interest. She's not sent the find signal, though, so whatever she's found, it's not Allen." He looked around and spotted two conference room chairs, both piled high with circuit boards and shrink-wrapped user manuals. "Can I move this junk onto the floor?"

She glanced back. "Sure, go for it." She watched while he emptied the chairs and dragged them across the room next to her. "What's this all about, anyway? It's pretty unusual to see Dr. Slytherin, I mean Sarnok, here in the lab doing actual work. Is Allen in trouble?"

"No, but we're not sure where he's at. This isn't your usual field test." Seth positioned the two chairs to face each other. He plopped down in one and put his feet up on the other. Ah, that was so much better.

"You mean he's missing," she murmured. "That doesn't sound good. That other guy, the hunky one in the black leather jacket? I got the idea he's a cop."

"Right you are. We're cooperating with the authorities to find Allen. Kind of a real-world test of her training."

"I bet he's Allen's new squeeze. He's sure butch enough." She chewed her lower lip. "Allen's not really missing, is he? I mean, he stopped by here yesterday afternoon." She tensed and her gaze locked on the screen. "Look, she's moving again."

Seth folded his hands over his belly and watched. Damn it, he needed a cigarette.

The door to the electronics lab slammed open. Dr. Sarnok stormed in and commanded, "I'm shutting this down right now."

Seth tilted an eyebrow at him. "We've just started. Teena's following the scent. Look." He pointed at the screen. "She's loping along at pretty good clip."

"I said shut this down. I just spoke with the mayor, and he's *incensed*. Incensed, I tell you. That detective person had no authority to initiate this search. The Chief Hartman is calling him right now to give him a good dressing down."

This could be serious. Maybe it was time to show his cards at last. Seth lowered his feet to the ground and sat up. "Look, you've had ants in your pants for weeks for a real-world test. The army's been all over you for results. This is your wet dream come true. Why shut it down?"

Sarnok turned purple. "Watch your tongue, Dr. Harzig. You'll show me due respect." He turned to Samantha. "You. Gomez. Break the connection with the specimen."

She turned to Seth and raised her eyebrows.

Sarnok stomped a foot. "Don't you look at him. Break the connection right *now*, or I'll destroy you."

Fucking bully. Time to give him some of his own back. "Samantha, do it. We can always reconnect later."

"But Dr. Harzig — "

"It'll be all right. Trust me. Shut it down and take a break in the coffee room. Dr. Sarnok and I need to talk."

She turned back to her screen and clicked the mouse. The doggie cursor vanished. "I'll be just down the hall if you need me." She glared at Sarnok and strode from the room, her back straight.

Sarnok turned a withering gaze on him. "How dare you defy me? You're fired. Don't go back to your office. Just leave."

"Now, now, Dr. Sarnok. I think you should reconsider. We really have some things we need to discuss."

Sarnok's eyes narrowed and his lips curled in a sneer. "Tell me about it. I know that you didn't destroy those early generation specimens. You filed false paperwork. I can prove it. That's scientific misconduct. Doubtless criminal fraud, too. You'll never work again."

Doubtless. What a phony jerk. The lab's phone rang and rang. Probably Sam calling in to find out what was going on.

Sarnok asked, "You going to answer that?"

Fuck him. Seth felt his pockets and found a pack of cigarettes. He pulled one out, lit it, and blew smoke in Sarnok's face.

"This is a non-smoking facility. Put that out."

"So what you going to do? Fire me?" His cell phone buzzed in his pocket. Probably Sam again. Ignore it for now. He looked around for an ash tray, and dug a used Styrofoam cup out of the waste basket. "You're right. I didn't destroy those dogs. They're intelligent. You made them that way. Destroying them is murder in my book."

Sarnok waved smoke away from his face. "They are experimental animals. You put them in the pound for adoption instead of doing your job. I can prove it. That runs the risk of polluting the local gene pool. I don't think anyone will sympathize with you, what with all the anti-GMO fools out there."

"I neutered the dogs first. No danger of pollution at all. Besides, if you go public with that, you'll have to tell them the dogs have *human* DNA in them. DNA *you* put there, without authorization from the NIH. If you shit-can me, you fuck yourself over, too. Think it through."

The man hooded his eyes, and his lips looked like he wanted to spit. "Maybe you're right. So you're not fired. Yet." Sarnok's jaw muscles jumped like he had a bit into a mouthful of grasshoppers. "But we still have to stop this test. The mayor was insistent. And you can't protect that loathsome detective. He's not even *from* here. He's not one of us. No one will care what happens to him."

Not one of us? That was dog-whistle for not white. Fucking assholes. "Well, *I* care." Seth licked his lips. *Time to turn the tables.* "Just why is the mayor so determined to stop this investigation?" He kept his voice smooth and low. Not threatening at all.

"He pointed out there would be a lot of publicity. It wouldn't be good for the city."

"But publicity *would* be good for you, wouldn't it? Brilliant scientist helps locate missing person, and all that." *Asshole. The most dangerous place in Hollenbeck is between you and a camera.*

"He appealed to my civic virtue." Sarnok's voice turned prim and his expression haughty. "He's got bigger ambitions than just being mayor of this small town, you know."

Seth stroked his upper lip to hide the incipient sneer that curled there. "Yeah. Tell me why would this would be bad for his political career? I don't get it."

"I really couldn't say. I'm a scientist and above such things. The important thing is that we've stopped this travesty."

"I think I know. I've been talking to Mrs. Bateman. She's got the most intriguing set of payroll records."

Sarnok paled. "I have no idea what you're talking about. And if she's been sharing confidential financial records with you, I'll fire her. You can't stop me."

"We're a public institution, remember? All it takes is a Freedom of Information request, and anyone can see them. They don't even have to say why. People might want to know why you've paid over six figures in consulting fees to the mayor and to the chief of police in the last year. Fuck, the army will want to know, too."

"Those are legitimate expenses." Despite his words, Sarnok's face turned the color of chalk.

Got him. "Well, then there's no problem, is there? Of course, the city might want to know why two of its senior employees had unreported outside income. But, since there's no problem, I'll just call my drinking buddy at the *Courier*. He's always looking for a tip." Seth pulled out his phone.

"Stop." Sarnok's face squirmed. His furrowed brow, compressed lips, and stylish stubble made him look more ferret-like than human. "Maybe we can come to an understanding. For the good of the project."

Seth's phone buzzed. He held it up and showed Sarnok the caller ID. "It's Detective Sondergard. What shall I tell him?"

"All *right*, already. Start the search back up. But you've got to agree to work with me. We've got to protect the project. Think of all the students and staff who work here."

Like you give a rat's ass about anyone but yourself. "We can talk. Later. Right now, I want you to go get Ms. Gomez and bring her back here. You can apologize to her in front of me and authorize her to reconnect with Teena."

"And you'll stay quiet?"

Seth considered. He'd gotten this far, but he hadn't planned for what came after. After all, he *had* falsified documents and released potentially dangerous experimental animals to the public. "I don't want to go to jail, either. I said we'd talk. We've got each other by the balls. Just don't forget it."

Sarnok's color returned to semblance of normal. His eyes narrowed, and his features hardened. "Very well, then. I trust you'll show me due respect, if for no other reason than appearances?"

What a scheming asshole. Like appearances mattered now. Seth shrugged. "Whatever. Get Ms. Gomez."

With Sarnok was gone, Seth texted Sam. *Temporary glitch. Back online soon.* That should hold him.

Sarnok led Samantha into the room. She had a sack of chips in one hand and a soda in the other. "What's up, Dr. Harzig?"

Seth turned to Sarnok and raised his eyebrows.

He cleared his throat. "Ahem. Yes, Ms. Gomez. Dr. Harzig has convinced me that it's in the best interests of the project to continue the test. You have my authorization to reconnect with specimen thirteen."

The weasel. "And?" Seth asked, his voice low.

"And I'm sorry if I was abrupt with you earlier. It was unprofessional of me." He turned to face Seth. "I'll leave this in your hands, Dr. Harzig. I have some calls I need to make."

Yeah. Run off and warn your cronies. "Of course, Dr. Sarnok. Just remember our shared interest in the success of this test."

Sarnok's eyes threw daggers at him. "I won't forget." He spun on his heel and left.

Samantha munched on chips and regarded him with somber eyes. "Wow. Just wow. What kind of spell did you cast on Dr. Slytherin?"

"I convinced him that this was the perfect opportunity to validate his work. Please. Reconnect with Teena."

"Sure thing, Doc." She slurped soda and plopped back down in front of her terminal. After a couple of clicks with the mouse, she frowned. "We've got a connection. Might take a minute to get the GPS data."

Seth stared at the monitor. No doggie cursor. "How long?"

"We should have it by now. Just a minute. Let me send a refresh command to the collar."

More clicks. A window popped up. *Acquiring satellites.* "It's re-synching with the satellites. We've got a good signal from the collar, just no GPS data."

"Is this normal?"

"Well, it's not *ab*normal. Usually it remembers satellite locations and re-synching is quick."

A new window popped up. *Satellites unavailable. Try again?*

Cold gripped Seth's gut. "What's that mean?"

"It can't find the satellites. Maybe she's indoors."

Another window popped up. *Target Found.*

Samantha's face lit up. "Look at that. She's sent the signal. That means she's found Allen. I knew she was good."

"But where is she? How long will it take to find her?"

"Oh. Well, if she's indoors, she'll never connect to the satellites. Ordinarily, we'd have a track to wherever she lost the GPS signal, but with the system shut off, all we've got is her last known location." She pointed to the screen. "Here, on Jenkins."

"So she could be anywhere. Is there any way to locate her without the GPS?"

"Hmm. I suppose if we had a mobile unit, we might be able to triangulate on her signal."

"Could you do that?"

"I don't see how. At least, not quickly. We're using military frequencies for the receiver here to talk to the collar, so I can't use commercial equipment to replicate this setup. That's why we relay via here to the mobile unit that cop's got, using standard cell phone connections." She frowned. "Maybe she'll go back outside. The GPS in the collar should reconnect pretty quickly if she does."

"Yeah. We told her to *hide*. She's not going anywhere." Seth slumped. So she's found Allen, but we have no way to know where. His phone buzzed. Sam calling again. What was he going to tell him?

Chapter 19

1806, Wednesday, October 31

Sam drummed his fingers against the steering wheel. The train clanked to a stop, then creaked and resumed its glacial progress. He peered at the SUV in front of him, and then twisted to look behind. Fuck. He was jammed in, no room to turn around. What to do?

His phone buzzed. A text from Harzig. What the fuck was a "temporary glitch?" Still no doggie-cursor on the tracking gizmo. He lit a cigarette and inhaled. It didn't help, and his car would stink tomorrow. Fuck it. Nothing mattered but finding Allen.

Wait. God damn, could that be the end of the train crawling into sight? It was. He snuffed the cigarette in the ashtray, flicked on his headlights, and swiped the wiper blades a couple of times. Afternoon was turning to twilight, and a light mist had started to fall. His Honda bounced over the tracks and he turned onto Jenkins. All he could think of to do was drive to the last good location he had on Teena.

The ragged edge of the Eagles Cemetery bounded the left side of Jenkins. Boarded-up warehouses hunkered on the other side. Soggy leaves and trash piled against the curb. Sam stopped at the corner of Jenkins and Fifth. Nothing. Fifth dead-ended in a dark loading dock a block away. No sign of Teena.

Time to call Harzig again. Voicemail. Fuck. He could at least answer.

His phone buzzed and he jumped. The Chief. Sam scowled. Maybe he should take the call. He didn't have anything better to do at the moment. "Sondergard here."

"Boy, what the Sam Hill are you doing? You get your ass into my office right now, you hear me?"

"Sir, I'm following a lead on the killer. I think I'm close to finding him. In fact — "

"I know what you're up to, boy. That professor fellow, Dr. Sarnok, he told me all about it, praise the Lord. What you *thinking,* letting that dangerous animal loose on the streets of my town?"

Sarnok? Of course. He'd *said* he had meetings today with the mayor. It made sense he'd brag to them about his research. Sam should have seen that coming. Stupid. "Sir, I'm convinced that a student at the college has been kidnapped by the killer. Teena's specially bred — "

"You just stop right there, boy. We don't need no police time spent looking for missing faggots. I've half a mind to suspend you."

Half a mind is an overestimate. "Sir, if I'm right we can catch the killer and close the investigation tonight."

"The only thing you're going to close is your career if you don't starting listening to me. I want you in my office with your files in thirty minutes. You got that, boy?"

Sam took a deep breath. *Fuck you and the horse you rode in on.* "Sir, I can't hear you. You're patching in and out. I think we've got a bad connection." He pressed end before the Chief could speak again.

Well, that burned that bridge. Now what? Without much hope, he tried the electronics lab. Surprise lifted his eyebrows when someone actually answered.

"Harzig here. Who's this?"

"Sondergard. What the fuck's going on? When will you get the signal back?"

"We've got it back — "

"No you don't. There's squat on my screen here."

"Let me finish, okay? We've reconnected with Teena's collar. She's *found Allen.* She's sent the signal. That's the good news."

Good news. That always meant there was bad news, too. He gritted his teeth. "So, where is he at?"

"That's the bad news. She must be inside a building. That will block the transmissions from the GPS satellites. We don't have any idea where she's at."

"So you're brilliant technology screwed up? That's just fucking perfect." *Sweet Jesus.*

"Listen to me. We know she's found him. It can't be far from her last known position. We were out of contact for less than thirty minutes. She's probably not more than half a mile from that."

Sam surveyed the shuttered buildings around him. "Great. That's probably over a hundred buildings to search, most of them locked up." He closed his eyes and tried to *think.* This couldn't be happening.

"Can't you organize a search or something, now that we've got it narrowed down?"

Right. The Chief wouldn't have done that *before*, and certainly not now. "Your boss Sarnok the Magnificent blabbed to the Chief about the search. He apparently made Teena sound slightly more dangerous than a rabid zombie with Ebola. He's probably going to fire me, and there's no fucking way he'll approve a search."

"That son of bitch," he whispered. Silence stretched. "What are you going to do?"

"I'm going to find Allen. One way or another."

"Well, we'll continue to monitor from here. If she goes back outside, we'll get a GPS signal. It'll show up on your monitor."

"Call me, too. I might not have the monitor with me."

"Will do. That SOB Sarnok. I promise you I'll get him for this."

"All I care about is rescuing Allen." Sam closed the connection and slumped in his seat. Visions of Allen's merry grin mixed with memories of Misha dying in his arms and Eric Bell's bloated body. That wasn't going to happen to Allen. It couldn't.

His windows fogged up, and he smeared the inside with his palm. He slid the car into gear and crept back onto Jenkins. Everything looked suspicious, but not enough to make him stop. He couldn't search dozens of buildings by himself.

His phone buzzed. It must be Harzig. "Is she back online? Where is she at?"

"Whoa, Sam. This is Amanda Mondrian. If this isn't a good time, I can call later."

He pulled to the curb and slammed on the brakes. "Dr. Mondrian. No, this is perfect. Were you able to pull anything from that SD card?"

"I'm still working on it. It's in pretty bad shape. So far I've only managed to reconstruct a couple of photos."

"They show anything?" Maybe he'd at last have a clue he could actually use.

"Let me send them to you. A text attachment okay?"

"Sure, sure. But tell me about them."

"One is a mangy-looking dog sitting in front of a blue van. No plates showing on the vehicle, but the right front fender is bashed in, if that's worth anything."

"It might be." At least it gave him something to look for instead of a random search. "What else?"

"The van's parked in front of a building. There's some faded lettering on the brick. I ran it through image enhancement, and it reads Klosuma. That's K-L-O-S-U-M-A.

The last letter could be an 'A' or a 'W,' but it's got to be an 'A.'"

"Why's that? I don't recognize it all."

"Klosuma's used to be a local chain of grocery stores. They all closed down about fifteen years ago."

"Was there one in the warehouse district off Jenkins?" It couldn't be that simple. Please, let it be that simple.

"Not that I recall. Why would anyone put a grocery store in the warehouse district?"

So much for that idea. "What else?"

"The other photo is pretty gruesome. I hope it's a still from a movie. *Hostel* maybe. It's a dismembered corpse on a stretcher."

Fuck. "It's probably real. Any identifying features? Can you tell where it might have been taken?"

"I was afraid it might be real. It's pretty fuzzy. Out of focus, and it looks like the lens was smeared. The same dog is in the picture, gnawing on a bone. I hate to think what *kind* of bone. But it just looks like a room. I'll keep running it through the enhancement program, but I don't have much hope."

"Well, it's something, that's for sure. Thank you, Dr. Mondrian."

Sam hung up and rubbed his chin. Damn. His fingers were trembling. Get a grip. You're not doing Allen any good by panicking. You've finally got a clue. Now what are you going to do with it?

His phone buzzed again, and he snatched it up. Not the Chief. Not Harzig, either. He frowned. The number was familiar. "Sondergard here. Talk to me."

"Sam, this is Otis."

Otis had lived in Hollenbeck like forever. Maybe he'd know something. "Have you ever heard of Klosuma's?"

"What? Yeah, it was a grocery chain. Sam, what's going on? The Chief's raging around, yelling he's going to fire your ass. I don't know what's set him off, but you need to be careful. I've never seen him so mad."

A little late for that warning. Not that he would have done anything different. "Fuck him. I'm close to finding the killer, Otis. This grocery chain. Did they have a store someplace in the warehouse district?"

"No. Wait. They had a *warehouse* there. Let me think. It's been years."

"It's important. This guy's kidnapped a new victim, a friend of mine from the college."

"Yeah. Hartman's been ranting about some kid at the college, calling him a faggot. Like that makes him less than human. What an ass hat." He paused, and then continued, "You know, I can visualize that warehouse. It was a couple stories tall, brick. It wasn't on Jenkins, though. Maybe Jefferson? I think that's right. Jefferson and Tenth."

"Fantastic. That helps more than you can know."

"Sam, what's this about? Are you planning to go there?"

He jerked his car from the curb and swerved. Headlights flashed a horn blared from a passing vehicle. That was close. "Yeah. I'm headed there now."

"You think the killer's there. Don't go in by yourself. You're going to need backup."

"Sure. I'll just call that right in to dispatch. I'm sure Chief'll see to it I get plenty of help."

"I told you I'd have your back. Give me thirty minutes. Don't go in alone."

"You don't have to risk your career for me. I'll be safe. Tell you what, I'll call you back if I find anything."

"I'm coming. Wait for me, damn it."

The phone fell silent, and Sam tossed his phone to the passenger seat. He had to admit he was glad Otis was coming.

He'd seen what happened to lone-wolf cops who went in without backup. Mostly they became dead cops.

He slowed as he turned onto Jefferson. Half the streetlights were broken, and his car jounced through the pot-holes that pocked the asphalt. Two warehouses stood between Tenth and Eleventh, separated by a narrow alley.

Sam caught his breath. There it was. A battered van hid in the depths between the buildings. He pulled up the image Dr. Mondrian had sent him. The dent in the fenders matched. This was it.

He drove on another thirty feet, pulled to the curb, and killed the engine. His kit was in the trunk. Kevlar vest, flashlight, Mossberg 500 pump-action shotgun. His Glock would be better for this, though. Too much danger of collateral damage from the Mossberg. He bit his lip and decided to carry the Mossberg after all, and keep his Glock at the ready in a holster at his hip. No telling what was inside, and the extra firepower of the shotgun might matter.

His preparations took seconds. He bent over and scrambled through the shadows to the van. It was dark inside, and the hood was cold. It stank, too. He recognized the odor. Dead body smell. The killer must have used it to transport corpses. This was the right place, for sure.

Just to be safe he flashed his light inside. God, what a filthy mess. Nobody there, though. Just trash.

Even in the gloom, he could make out the faded red paint on the building on his left. Klosuma's Warehouse. Wooden stairs rose from the alley to a metal door on the second floor. The first riser was broken, but his flashlight revealed a muddy footprint on the second. The killer had to be up there. The door at the top was ajar, and faint light leaked from the edges.

The rain was falling harder now, drumming against the pavement and rooftops. Sam hunched against the cold. Otis was right. He really shouldn't go in without backup. He thought about lighting a cigarette.

A muffled scream, faint but unmistakable, floated through the alley, its sound gossamer as a spider's web. Icicles stabbed Sam in the gut. Another scream rose and ended in sobs. Whatever was happening up there couldn't wait.

He gripped the Mossberg and ascended the stairs.

Chapter 20

1900, Wednesday, October 31

Fatigue pummeled Allen's body. Every joint ached. He couldn't remember sleeping, but he must have drifted off. How long had he been here? Days? He shook his head to clear his thoughts, but that only brought more pain, as though his brain was too big for his skull. Each heartbeat sent blood slamming through his head in pulsing agony.

Candles flickered everywhere. Dozens of them, on the floor, on tables, on the shelves, sending insane shadows racing across the room. Pete, poor Pete. He was still bound to the stretcher. A crusty trail of dried blood ran from above his ear, down his temple, to a dark puddle on the floor. Dozens of angry bruises and tiny gashes peppered his body. His head flopped to one side, and he gazed at Allen from sunken eyes bereft of hope.

Allen heaved a shuddering breath and glanced at his own body. We must look the same. Horror shows.

The tinny sound of a TV cop show rattled from the next room. Bobby must be watching *Law and Order* again. Yeah. That was the theme that *clanged, clanged*, and light from the screen scintillated through the doorway.

When will this be over? Just stop. Kill me now. I don't care.

The TV sounds stopped and the music started again. The Platters. Bobby had a thing for oldies. *Smoke Gets in Your Eyes*. Allen's heart was on fire, once, for Sam. That was before Bobby. That was outside this hell, in the real world. Now the universe consisted of fear. Pain, too, but mostly fear.

Sam. The time for their dinner date must have come and gone. What would he be thinking? He's probably decided I stood him up. Broke up with him.

That fight was so stupid. Now I'll never be able to make up with him. Tell him how I really feel.

He'd been doing something before, before he fell asleep. Something important. What was it?

Movement caught his eye. Bobby was back.

He swayed into the room, circling in a slow tango with an invisible partner. Spot trotted after him and headed to a dark corner. He circled three times, and then settled, head on paws. Allen blinked, and the dog disappeared in the shadows. Only his eyes, red in the reflected glow of the candles, remained visible.

Bobby's dance stopped at the table next to Pete. The table with the torture instruments. He put a finger to his cheek and tipped his head. "What do you think, my pretty?" He picked up a corkscrew and showed it to Pete. "This looks interesting, don't you think?"

Pete squeezed his eyes closed and squirmed on the table. The only sounds that could come from behind the duct tape around his head were grunts and groans.

Bobby's features twisted into an angelic smile. "What's that, my pretty? I can't hear you." He put the corkscrew down and picked up the scalpel. The blade glimmered red in the candlelight.

Pete's muffled screams grew more frantic.

Allen twisted in his chair. His left wrist *moved.* That was what he'd been doing. Working his wrist. Fighting back.

Maybe, just maybe, he could do something while Bobby was occupied. It *was* looser. With just a little more work, maybe he could free it. The muscles cramped but he kept at it. He imagined tearing one wrist free, then the other. Quietly, stealthily, while Bobby focused on Pete. He'd sneak up behind him. Slit the bastard's throat with his own fucking knife.

Bobby reached out and touched his index finger where Pete's lips would be under the tape. "Hush, now." He hummed off key with the music. "I think you're trying to tell me something. Shall we take off this tape?"

Pete just stared at him with vacant eyes.

"Yes, I think that's what we'll do." He reached out and feathered the blade under the duct tape near Pete's jaw.

Allen wrenched his wrist and it *rotated.* It was definitely looser.

The music stopped. Somewhere, a faucet dripped. The windows rattled in a gust of wind. Spot whimpered from his corner, and his tail thumped against the floor.

Pete screamed.

Allen lurched his attention back to Bobby and his victim. Pete's mouth was finally free. But Bobby had slit Pete's cheek. Stubble darkened his craggy features, but now blood flowed from a gash that ran from his cheekbone to his jaw, just to the left of his mouth.

Pete screamed again, and blood sprayed.

Bobby picked up a squeeze bottle and squirted a colorless liquid on the wound.

Pete's body writhed and his shrieks grew louder, more frantic.

Bobby had used the spray on Allen earlier. He'd made criss-cross cuts on Allen's nipples, and then sprayed them with liquid fire.

Allen twisted his wrist back and forth and tugged. His hand *almost* would slip between the tape and the arm of the chair. Just a few more seconds. One way or another, his nightmare was going to end.

Bobby murmured to Pete, "Hush, hush, my pretty. It's just alcohol, cayenne pepper, and vinegar. It'll stop the bleeding." He stroked Pete's brow. "You should rest." He dropped the squeeze bottle onto the table and picked up a syringe. While he held it up and tapped the tube, he murmured, "Close your eyes, now, and rest." He jabbed the needle into Pete's neck.

Pete's eyes bulged and tendons and veins outlined his tortured torso. In seconds his eyes fluttered and closed.

Bobby stroked Pete's brow. "Don't worry, my sweet. I'll play with you again, later."

Icy knives of fear stabbed Allen's gut. Playing with Pete later meant it was Allen's turn. He jerked his arm. Almost free.

Bobby sauntered across the room and gazed at Allen with hooded eyes. "What are you doing with that arm, my precious?"

Allen froze. His throat clenched.

Bobby twirled the scalpel in his fingers. But then he pulled a tool off the wall behind Allen. A hammer.

No, no, no. What was he going to do?

The hammer bashed into Allen's wrist. Agony lacerated his arm and blackness edged his vision. Futile screams tore at his throat, squelched by the duct tape about his mouth. Dreams of escape vanished like smoke, replaced by despair.

A voice from nowhere shouted, "Police. Drop your weapon."

What was that? Was it from the television?

A figure emerged from the darkness, dressed in black. He carried a shotgun in one hand and a handgun in the other. "Drop your weapon. Now."

Sam. It was Sam, come to rescue him. How did he get here?

Bobby scuttled out of Allen's sight. Something sharp pricked against his throat, and Bobby's foul breath heated his neck. "You drop yours, or I'll slit this one's jugular."

Allen held his breath. Don't drop your gun, Sam. Don't do it. Kill the bastard.

Sam's face turned to stone. His shotgun clunked to the floor, but he gripped his handgun with both fists and pointed at Allen. "You touch him and I'll blow your brains out. Drop the knife and we'll work this out. You don't have to die."

Bobby's suave voice grew an edge. "Drop your gun. Think about it." He snatched at Allen's hair and twisted his head back. "When you cut the jugular, the blood jets out, sometimes as much as twenty feet. It'll feel warm when it splashes against your face." He snickered. "Think you're ready for that? You could lick it off your lips. What will it taste like?"

The pressure against Allen's neck increased. His whole body quaked, helpless. His eyes never left Sam. Shoot him. Don't drop your gun. *Shoot him.*

Sam's gun wavered. "Don't cut him."

Bobby howled with laughter.

The pressure on Allen's neck increased and *burned.*

Sam's gun flashed. Blinding fire erupted from the muzzle.

Something hot and wet splattered against Allen's cheek. Had Bobby done it? Had he cut Allen's throat? Had Sam missed?

The pressure at Allen's neck released. Bobby thudded to the floor, where he lurched and then fell still. The back of his head was missing.

Sam's fingers probed Allen's neck where the scalpel had just been. "Babe, babe. It's all right. Just a nick. Like shaving. You're going to be fine." He pointed to Bobby. "He can't hurt you anymore. I blew the bastard's brains out." He squatted down and laid his handgun on the floor at Allen's feet while he pried the scalpel from Bobby's fingers. "Let me get you free."

With gentle fingers, he sawed through the tape around Allen's mouth. "This will smart. I'm going to pull it off all at once."

It didn't smart. It felt wonderful. Free. Allen sucked in gulps of air. Sam should help Pete. He hadn't moved during any of this. Allen tried to tell Sam, but all that came out were croaking sounds. He hadn't had anything to drink since Bobby had taken him. His throat felt like he'd been gargling boiling acid.

Sam continued to saw at Allen's bonds. His arms were free. Now his legs. It was wonderful. He tried to stand. He wanted to kick Bobby, he needed to kick him. But his legs wouldn't hold him and he collapsed into Sam's strong arms.

"That's all right, Babe. I've got backup coming." He glanced at Pete. "I need to call for an ambulance and see to the other guy." He helped Allen to the floor, slipped off his leather jacket, and covered Allen's nakedness. "Rest, babe. It's going to be all right. You're safe."

Safe. Would he ever feel safe again? Even with Bobby's lifeless body right next to him, his dead eyes staring at nothing, fear still jittered in his heart. He was forgetting something. Something important. Not his wrist. Fuck. It was swollen to twice its normal size and hurt like fury.

What was he forgetting?

Across the room, a pair of candles moved. No. Not candles. Eyes. Spot crept forward. His mouth foamed, and his eyes locked on Sam.

That was what he forgot. Spot. A second generation CHIP, and dangerous as hell. He had to warn Sam. He opened his mouth, but nothing came out. He tried to swallow, but his mouth was dry. He pounded on the floor, but he was too weak to get Sam's attention.

Spot's muscles tensed, and a silent snarl curled his lips.

Sam's fingers shook when punched his cell phone. "Karen. I need a wagon right away. Two civilians down. I'm at — "

Spot launched himself, a coiled ball of canine muscle and teeth. He struck Sam from behind. His phone flew from his hand and clattered across the floor. Spot's momentum bowled him over. He slammed to the floor and his head struck the hardwood with a crack.

He stopped moving.

Spot tore into him, going for the throat but instead ripping into the dark blue vest he was wearing. Blood flowed from Sam's shoulder.

What to do? Allen forced himself to sit up. His hand brushed against something hot. Sam's gun. Fuck, it was heavy. It sagged in his fist. He pointed it at Spot, but didn't fire. What if he hit Sam instead? He didn't know anything about guns.

From nowhere, another snarling dog appeared. Two dogs? Bobby had *two* CHIP dogs?

Wait. The second dog attacked *Spot*. It — no, she — she grabbed Spot by the throat and dragged him off Sam. It was all happening too fast. The two animals intertwined. Growls mixed with howls. Spot broke free and they circled each other, baring their teeth.

Allen lifted the gun again. They were away from Sam. He could fire now.

The new dog wore a tag. She was another CHIP for sure. What was *she* doing here? It didn't matter. She must have reverted to feral, like Spot, to be so ferocious. He had to protect Sam. He raised the gun and pulled the trigger. Fire bloomed from the muzzle. But it didn't fire just once. He couldn't tell how many, but at least a dozen shots thundered from the weapon.

The gun kicked and flew from his hand. It slammed into his wrist and he screamed in pain.

But the dogs were silent. They lay twisted together. Spot's head was mostly missing, but the new one still twitched. She raised her head and *nodded* at him. Then her eyes closed and she relaxed, as if in sleep.

What had he *done?* It suddenly all fell in place. The new dog was *Teena. That* was how Sam found him. *She* had found him, and led Sam to him. She wasn't feral — she'd been *rescuing* Sam.

And now he'd killed her.

A siren sounded in the distance. Sam and Pete still didn't move. Neither did Teena. Allen tried to crawl to Sam, to Teena, but something snapped in his arm and searing pain delivered him to unconsciousness.

Epilogue

1500, Friday, May 10

Allen rubbed his wrist and paced in the hallway outside the zoology department's seminar room. He really shouldn't be nervous about his dissertation defense, but the Dean Griffin's offhand joke about how "these things almost always turn out well" wasn't exactly a confidence builder.

Sam lounged on a stiff-backed bench and regarded him with an amused expression. "Stop it. They *said* you did fine."

"You weren't there when they closed the defense for questions." Allen plopped down next him and wished for caffeine.

"Didn't you answer them?"

"Well, yeah. But what's taking them so long?"

"Don't be such a worry-wart. They're probably sitting around planning their next department beer bash. Stop being so nervous. Everything will work out."

"But the job at Montgomery College is contingent on my having earned the doctorate. All our plans — "

"I think they'll cut you some slack at Montgomery. That trustee, Sandra Montgomery, she *likes* you. She likes both of us. She saw to it they had a job for me, too, after you applied there. The college is named for her father, for God's sake. They're not going take your job or mine away over a little thing like a defense."

"It's *not* a little thing." *Damn it, he gets to be chief of security at Montgomery. I don't want to be some flunky failure of an adjunct professor.*

The door opened, and Dr. Eckhorn stuck her nose out. "Allen? Will you please step inside?"

She wasn't smiling. Was that a bad sign? But she never smiled. With butterflies dancing in his belly, Allen followed her back into the seminar room.

The Dean stood, his face grave. "Let me be the first to congratulate you, Dr. LeClerc." He thrust out his hand.

Allen wobbled on unsteady legs. *Doctor* LeClerc. Yay! He'd *passed.* "Thank you, Dean Griffin. I couldn't have finished if you hadn't helped." The Dean seemed to want to pull his arm off. At least it wasn't his left arm, which was still sore from physical therapy this morning. But then, it didn't matter. He'd *passed.*

"You did the work, Dr. LeClerc. Brilliant work it is, too, I have to say. It's especially a credit to your ability that you persevered even after Dr. Sarnok, uh, decided to pursue other opportunities."

Other opportunities. Right. The trial on misappropriation of funds wasn't scheduled yet, but Dr. Sarnok's 'other opportunities' probably involved a few years of making license plates for the state. The SOB.

Dr. Eckhorn gave him a limp handshake. "Good work, Allen. It's a shame the Army has placed an embargo on your research. Your techniques working with interspecies DNA are ground-breaking."

"Your application of positive psychology to animal training is at least as impressive." Dr. Harzig clasped him on the shoulder. "Good job, Allen. Tell us your plans. What's next?"

"Well, you know I've accepted an offer from Montgomery College in Wisconsin. They've agreed to set up a canine research facility for me so I can continue my work. My husband has a job with them, too, as chief of security for the campus."

Dr. Harzig nodded. "You and Sam are a good match. I'm glad the new Chief of Police reinstated him after what the old chief tried to pull. What was the asshole thinking, firing him after that heroic rescue?"

Allen didn't want to think about that day. "Well, it's all worked out." It had been pretty bad for a while. Allen had been in the hospital for weeks. That jerk Sarnok tried to kick him out of school, and the Chief of Police had fired Sam for an "unauthorized investigation." But then, out of nowhere, Sarnok resigned and the mayor left to take a job with a Fox TV franchise upstate. Dean Griffin took over as Allen's dissertation advisor. The City Council fired Chief Hartman and named Lizzie's husband to the post. Sam said everything would work out, and he'd been right.

Harzig babbled on. "Still, it's a shame you're leaving Hollenbeck. Our community could use more folks like the two of you. With a new city administration, things are looking up."

Allen put a grim smile on his face. "Like I said, it's all worked out. Otis treated Sam right, that's for sure. He and his wife are good people." He brightened. "They're having a reception at Smithson Green for us at five. Everyone is welcome."

Dean Griffin said, "I've come to know Mrs. Bateman well over the last few months. Browning is fortunate to have her as an employee."

He harrumphed and changed the subject. "I've heard of Montgomery College, Allen. That's an excellent little school. Hefty endowment, and it has highly selective admissions. You've done well and been a credit to Browning. We're all proud of you." He glanced at his watch. "I enjoyed your defense. Congratulations again, but I have to run. I'll try to stop by your party."

The dissertation committee scattered and Allen bounced into the hall. "I passed," he announced to Sam.

"I could tell. Your smile is so wide you had to go through the door sideways."

"Ha ha. Very funny."

"You ready? We need to head out to Otis's and Lizzie's party. They've got a cake and everything to celebrate."

Allen heaved a deep breath. "Come here, you. Give me a hug. I wouldn't even be here if you hadn't saved my life." He melted into Sam's strong embrace and steel-hard body.

Sam pulled back and pecked him on the lips. "We saved each other, actually. That damned dog Spot would have torn me to shreds."

Allen's lips turned down. "Spot." He shuddered. "Teena's the one who saved you from him. I wouldn't have a dissertation if it weren't for her. If she hadn't found me, you couldn't have saved me, and we wouldn't be married." He stopped and bit his lip. "And for all of that, I shot her."

Sam squeezed him. "Stop guilting yourself. This is a day to be happy, not for regrets. Come on. Trisha's waiting outside with her van to take us to the party."

Allen let Sam lead him down the hall and into the spring sunshine. Trisha's face split into a grin, and she waved to them from where she stood in the parking lot. "You boys look happy," she called. "I suppose that means things went well."

Allen waved and shouted back, "Terrific, Trisha."

He ran ahead.

Trisha's arm jerked and she released the leash holding back Teena. Allen's best friend scampered up to him and nosed his pocket.

Allen grinned, tousled her ears, and let her lick a doggie treat from his palm. He stroked her side, and his fingers ran over the scars on her body that the bullets had left. At least she'd recovered, and the College had given her to him, thanks to Dr. Harzig.

He gripped her leash with one hand and took Sam's hand with the other. Two men and their dog, together.

Life was good.

About the Author

Max writes horror and science fiction stories, often with a dark twist. John Gardner's *The Art of Fiction* is the single most important influence on his thinking about the craft of writing. Authors as diverse as John Updike, Dean Koontz, Richard Matheson, and Lawrence Block inspire and inform his literary style.

Max Griffin is the pen name of a mathematician and academic. Under his professional name, he is the author of a graduate textbook in real analysis and numerous research articles in nonlinear functional analysis. When he is not writing fiction, his days are filled with teaching mathematics and statistics, research, and administrative work at a major comprehensive university in the southwest. He is the proud parent of a daughter who is a librarian, and the grandparent to two beautiful, little boys. He is blessed to be in a long-term relationship with his life partner, Mr. Gene, who is an expert knitter.

The two humans in Max's household are the pets of an Abyssinian cat named Mr. Dinger, short for Erwin Schrodinger the Cat. Mr. Dinger graciously lets them live in his home in return for food and occasional petting. Oh, and there's that litter box thing they do for him, too.

Visit him online at www.MaxGriffin.net

PURPLE SWORD PUBLICATIONS
www.purplesword.com